CAN'T MAKE YOU LOVE ME

LIBBY WATERFORD

ALSO BY LIBBY WATERFORD

Sawyer's Cove: The Reboot

Take Two

Take a Bow

Take it All

Take a Chance

Hot Take in Steamy Shorts: A Kissed by Romance Anthology

Take Another Look in A Kiss at Midnight: A Kissed by Romance Collaboration

Never a Bride

Can't Help Falling in Love

Can't Make You Love Me

Can't Fight This Feeling

Can't Hurry Love

Weston Reunion

Flirting with Her Professor

Her Reunion Fling

Falling for Her Ex

For Pippa

CHAPTER 1

OPHELIA'S INBOX

From: Nicole Winesap <nicole@winesap.design>
To: Rosie Snyder <r_snyder@venturahospital.org>; Kate Treanor <kate@treanorpod.com>; Lani Kalama <lani@winesap.design>; Ophelia Winesap <o.winesap@clintonelemen.edu>

Subject: Bachelorette Party—Mandatory!!

Hey you Beautiful Badass Bridesmaids!

I've given you all enough time to recover from the holidays and now we get to start thinking about the bachelorette. Kate and Rosie are taking the lead on this one, so listen to them and do whatever they say, but consider this your save the date so no one makes ANY plans for the three days in April that we're going to be celebrating.

And don't forget—this is a GIRLS ONLY event. No boys allowed! That means you, Rosie! Your hottie boyfriend will need to find alternate entertainment for the weekend.

However, dates are *encouraged* (but not mandatory) for the

wedding, so don't forget to add your plus-ones when you fill out your RSVP cards in a couple months!

Kisses,
Nicole

CHAPTER 2

OPHELIA

In the six minutes before Mrs. Lake's fourth grade class arrives I check my email and immediately regret it: another wedding-related missive from Santa Barbara's biggest Bridezilla, my cousin Nicole Winesap.

She's five years older than I am and basically my big sister, which is why I agreed to be her maid of honor. But none of us bridesmaids could have predicted exactly how hands-on she'd be about this wedding. She's orchestrating and planning everything like it's a war campaign.

Nor could we predict how weird she'd get about our love lives, specifically, wanting to see the four of us settled down with the loves of our lives immediately, or sooner if possible. We even started a support group to help us make it to the big day without strangling dear Nicole.

I switch apps and see there's already chatter among the Never a Bride(smaids) about the latest email. Some of my anxiety bleeds away. I may be a little younger than the other three, but they've become friends as we've gone through these epic wedding preparations together. We've all bonded over not wanting to spend our lives chasing some mythical happily ever after.

KATE

Don't worry, ladies. Rosie & I aren't planning
anything too wild for this bachelorette thing.
The craziest part about it is that it's going to
be 3 freaking days long

LANI

How many days do we really need?

ROSIE

However many days Nicole tells us we need,
of course 😜

I smile and stash my phone as the fourth graders file in. I'm in my third year as head librarian at Clinton Elementary School, so I've known these kids since they were tiny little second graders. Now some of them are almost as tall as I am. Not hard, since I barely top five feet.

They're deep in the middle of their California history unit, which means lots of research and nonfiction reading. It's tough on some of the kids who are only into wizards or mermaids, but it's good for them to stretch. One of my favorite parts of the job is pushing kids out of their reading comfort zones and watching them discover new passions.

Ingrid, the assistant librarian, helps the kids find books that will aid them in their mandatory mission projects: building a diorama of one of California's twenty-one missions.

"Can we use the maker lab today, Miss Winesap?" Jewel asks. She's been assigned Mission San Buenaventura and she's designing the façade on our MakerBot Replicator Mini 3D printer.

"Not today, Jewel. You can come in during open hours on Monday, or you can arrange to come in after school next week if you need more time."

"I wish I could work on my design at home," she says.

"You know what? I'll ask my friend Jamie if he knows of a

way for you to do that, then you can do the fabrication part in the lab."

"Thanks, Miss Winesap!" Her spirits are immediately restored, and I hope that Jamie Kendell can come up with a solution.

Jamie and I piloted the maker lab for my elementary students in a converted closet in my already too-small library. It has four 3D printers and the attendant accessories, like the plastic filament that the printers use to create 3D objects out of tiny layers, based on designs the kids create on the connected computer. The lab opened in the fall to much fanfare, and the kids love it. It makes them feel like inventors and explorers, which they naturally are. I wish we could set up labs in every school in the district.

I bring my idea up with Jamie later, at our standing lunch date in the pocket park near the museum where he works. The Fox Museum of Science and Innovation at Santa Barbara, The Fox for short, sits on a prime piece of real estate three blocks from the waterfront, and a mere half-mile from my school. We meet for lunch two or three times a week, with the ocean on one side of us and the sage green mountains against which our hometown is nestled on the other.

"Do you think it's worth talking to Mihret?" I ask around bites of my wrap. Jamie's boss, the museum's CEO, was instrumental in getting our lab off the ground. "We could try to get funding to expand the program."

"Definitely. We always hoped to take the model wider, and you've been doing some amazing stuff with your students. That rocket ship the third graders built was out of this world." Jamie smiles at me, and for a second I'm distracted—he's got one of the greatest smiles ever—generous lips curving to reveal even white teeth. Then I recover and laugh.

"You are such a dork."

"Thank you," he says with mock seriousness. He bites into

an apple and says with his mouth half-full, "I'll email you some online design resources your fourth graders can use for their mission projects."

"Thanks." He's unfailingly good to me and to the kids we both work with, despite his table manners. We're not technically at a table, but still.

"In other news, Nicole's already sending emails about the bachelorette party and it's not for three months," I whine.

Jamie rolls his eyes. "Jesus. I don't understand why we're on the hook for party after party. I thought you got one day—the wedding. So far we've had the engagement party, next you have the bachelorette. She's probably going to want some shower thing, too."

"I'm with you." Nicole is marrying Jamie's cousin Ricky, which is how Jamie and I met. "But just think, they're both only children, like us. If they don't do it up, there might not be another wedding in the Winesap-Kendell family for a generation. God knows I won't be having one."

A silence descends, not exactly uncomfortable, but not easy. I say, "The rain held off," to fill the gap.

"Yeah, it's supposed to start during rush hour. Traffic is going to be rough later," Jamie says, finishing his apple in two more bites.

"Are you going somewhere?"

"Ricky and I are heading to L.A. for a couple nights. Going to that maker conference I told you about."

"Oh yeah. I forgot. I was going to ask if you wanted to go to the superhero movie that we never got around to seeing during the holidays. It's still playing in Goleta."

"Can we do it when I get back? Sunday night?"

"Sure." I swallow the unexpected pang of disappointment at not getting to see him until then.

He glances at his phone. "Hey, if you have a minute, want to walk me back? I could show you our new soldering irons."

"I have some time." The school usually holds assemblies on Friday afternoon, so I don't have to be back for any classes, just to tidy the loose ends of the week before heading home.

We gather our things and slip into The Fox through the service entrance, surprising some docents on their break as we walk through to the museum's maker space, which is five times the size of mine. It has larger, more sophisticated computers and printers, and also wiring and soldering equipment for electrical experiments, molds for small-scale metal casting, and low-tech paper, scissors, glue, and markers.

"Hey, Jamie." A young woman with curly brown hair greets us inside the maker space.

"Hey, Alanna. You remember Ophelia?" Alanna is the director of programs. She zooms around the museum's three floors of interactive exhibits making sure everything runs like clockwork.

"Sure, hey." We exchange waves. "You need anything for your two o'clock demo?"

"No, I think I'm good. I've got two volunteers assigned to this room, right?"

"Chase and Danielle S.," Alanna says.

"Is Danielle S. the one with the service dog?" Jamie asks.

"No, that's Danielle C. She's not in today."

"Bummer. I love lecturing the kids on not petting a service animal. I'll just have to do it another time."

Alanna laughs. "You'll have your hands full with thirty first graders, anyway. They're on the roof right now, but you better get ready." She moves away toward the wind tunnel exhibit and Jamie winces.

"This musical instrument unit has been a little...noisy. I can't wait until we move on to coin making. Much easier on the ears."

"But more burn danger," I say.

Jamie lets out a short laugh. I love making him laugh. I

watch him move through the space as if he's at home. He pulls out a box of tools and holds one up. "Speaking of burn danger, here are the soldering irons. Cool, huh?"

"Yeah, very cool." I don't know a soldering iron from a curling iron. My straight blonde hair doesn't hold curls easily.

"Hey, Jamie!" A teenager wearing the light blue volunteer T-shirt appears at our side. "Wow, soldering irons!"

"Hey, Chase," Jamie says. "Can you do thirty setups of the drum project, please?"

"Sure, Jamie. On it," Chase says eagerly.

I'm always surprised at how much of a rock star Jamie is here. The smaller kids respond to his energy like he's Inventor Elmo or something, and the teenagers either want to be just like him or want his attention. Even the older docents act differently around him than the other staff. Some of the girls fluff their hair and touch his arm. Some of the boys straighten their glasses and adjust their posture.

When I'm with Jamie and other people, it reminds me what a catch he is. For someone else. He's smart, obviously. Good-looking in an approachable way. The museum's signature blue shirt that he invariably wears paired with jeans and Chucks effortlessly sets off his blue-green eyes, even if they are framed by rectangular black-rimmed glasses. Today he looks as though it's been a few days since he's shaved, but I personally like him without any stubble to detract from his full, sculpted mouth. It's the mouth, I think, that really grabs the attention. It looks made for kissing. And since kissing always seems to be the last thing on his tremendously talented mind, that makes the challenge all the sweeter.

Not for me, of course.

I might care if any of these groupies made it past the museum's doors with him, out into the world where I'd have to interact with them on a regular basis. But since Jamie and his last girlfriend, Kara, broke up about a year ago, he hasn't dated anyone—that I know of.

Technically, I wouldn't know, because the topic of relationships is completely off-limits between the two of us. I don't want to know and he doesn't tell me. It makes it easy to forget that I don't actually have any claim to him outside of our friendship or almost-familial status. I don't need him to belong to me that way.

Though I can't deny it's nice that he doesn't belong to anyone else that way, either.

"I better get back to work. Have fun with the drums," I say, backing away slowly.

"See you Sunday, Ophelia." His eyes move off his work and back to me, and I feel that electric pulse of having his attention all to myself again. It's kind of addictive.

"See you then." I escape before I turn into another Jamie Kendell groupie.

CHAPTER 3

JAMIE

After the first grade field trip files out of the maker space, each student clutching a small drum made from paper, glue, and Popsicle sticks—hey, not all creation has to be high tech—I clean up the lab.

I tidy each workstation, brush bits of plastic molding into the recycle bin, and reset the demos. I put away the new soldering irons, smiling at the memory of Ophelia trying to conjure up some enthusiasm for the tools. I know she doesn't share my gadget fetish, but it was the first thing that popped into my head when I was trying to come up with a reason to extend our lunch date.

I've been doing that all the time lately—looking for reasons to hang out more, talk longer. Not that we need a special reason. We're friends. Practically best friends, she'd say. We spend plenty of time together. Which is why it's embarrassing to admit how long it took me to reject the idea of blowing off Ricky and our long-scheduled weekend plans just to take Ophelia to the movies. The movie will still be playing Sunday, and O will still be there to go with.

I lock the lab a few minutes after the museum closes and

check the weather app on my phone for the tenth time today. The predicted rain hasn't started yet, which is a small mercy. Any amount of winter precipitation tends to throw sun-loving Santa Barbara into a panic. I'll pick up Ricky at his office on upper State Street before we swing south toward Los Angeles. Just where I want to be during Friday rush hour—sitting in bumper-to-bumper traffic on the 101. But we're expected at the conference, and Ricky and I don't get to spend much time together without Nicole and Ophelia around.

Maybe a couple days away from O will be good for me, clear my head a little.

I tell myself it's not pathetic that the woman I think about all the time isn't my girlfriend. Spending time with my favorite woman in the world is what's important. Not the fact that we're not in a physical relationship, and never will be. What matters is that I'm happy when I'm with her, and I think I make her happy, too.

Today's lunch is case in point—she was already at our bench and didn't notice me right away, so I had a moment to admire her in a way that I try to keep as platonic as possible. She's beautiful, but she doesn't want me to see her like that. So I pretend when I'm with her that I don't notice her heart-shaped face, her flawless skin, her always slightly messy bun of dark blonde hair.

There I go again. I need to get her out of my head. I slide behind the wheel of my black Volkswagen GTI, set my speakers to blasting, and let Radiohead block out any thoughts of pretty blonde cousins-in-law-to-be.

* * *

The second day of the conference Ricky and I grab lunch at a taco truck in Grand Park. I'm pumped up on the stuff we've seen demoed, and I'm itching to get back to my shop and try out some new tweaks on the printer I'm designing.

"It's happening, man," I say to Ricky between bites of carnitas. "We're going to be making 3D printers with 3D printers. Someday everyone's going to have one in their kitchen, just like we're all starting to have those creepy voice command speakers."

"Hey, my digital assistant is not creepy. She's helpful. How else would I find out the weather forecast while shaving?"

"Dude, the fact that you call it a 'she' is creepy enough. And we live in Southern California. The weather is not that complicated."

Ricky shrugs. "We get weather."

"Whatever, imagine if everyone in the world had the ability to make their own replacement parts for their appliances, or design and build their own appliance from scratch? We'd be a planet of people who can make the things they need instead of buying them. It will be like preindustrial society except instead of needing to specialize with one ironmonger, one blacksmith, one carpenter, each person can have all of those specialties at their fingertips."

"I don't see how having a device that can make anything you can think of is any less creepy than a digital voice that tells you the time and the Dodgers score. People could make—I don't know—weapons. It sounds like it would threaten our way of life."

Ricky's a venture capitalist and the poster boy for capitalism, even if he does try to use his power for good. "Don't worry, there will still be a free market. We'll need to buy materials to use in the printers—until someone figures out a way to turn household waste into useable material, that is." I grin at him.

"If this is going to be as much of a revolution as you think, I want in on the ground floor."

"Naturally."

I want to make it happen faster and cheaper. I want everyone to have one of my small, quick, light, user-friendly 3D printers in their homes, schools, and offices. It's a weird dream, but it's mine. I've made enough progress on a simpler printer design that my manufacturing partner has been able to make some viable prototypes. If my designs hold up and we can get the proper manufacturing in place, these machines will be one step closer to a printer that would be able to make a replica of itself. And that would be fucking awesome.

Ricky glances at his phone. A familiar dopey smile spreads on his face, and I know he's gotten a message from his fiancée. He types out a quick text and I try not to be jealous. It's been a year since I had a girlfriend, and I kind of miss it. The little things like texting and jokes and movies. And the not-so-little things, like sex. Come to think of it, I have all those things with Ophelia. Except the sex, of course.

"I'm catching a movie with O tomorrow when we get back. You and Nicole want to come?"

Ever since Nicole and Ricky moved back to Santa Barbara after years in New York, the four of us have gotten pretty tight. Nicole and Ricky, Ophelia and me. Two sets of cousins. Two sets of friends. One couple. One...non-couple. It's fine. Since Nicole and O are as close as sisters, and Ricky and I are as close as brothers, maybe that makes O and me siblings by proxy. And you don't have aching, intense fantasies about your sibling. So we're good. Totally.

"Nah. I better rest up before work. I think Nicole has some design podcast she's recording with Kate."

"No worries." As much fun as we have when we hang out as a foursome, I like having Ophelia to myself. In my more pathetic moments I can pretend we're on a date and our banter is really flirtation.

Torture myself, in other words.

"We should get back if we're going to catch that lecture on voice-recognition software."

"Let's do this," Ricky says, tossing his taco wrapper in the trash.

I nudge my glasses up the bridge of my nose and try to forget about Ophelia for a little while longer.

CHAPTER 4

OPHELIA

"You will not believe what my mom thought about the bridesmaid dresses I showed her," Nicole says as the server at our favorite brunch place on State Street refills our iced teas. The rain that's fallen steadily since Friday afternoon is still coming down Sunday morning.

"Let me guess—she hated them?" I bite into my chocolate chip scone, which arrived before the eggs Benedict I ordered. Eating dessert first is not exactly against my values, but I still feel a little guilty about putting the baked good ahead of protein.

Nicole, naturally, didn't order anything sweet. She's on a mission to look '90s fashion-model slender for her wedding. She has the willpower for that kind of sacrifice. I do not. Yet another reason that being single is pretty damn fabulous. I don't have anyone telling me not to eat carbs. Except Nicole, of course.

"She *hated* them." No surprise. Nicole and her mom, my aunt Sandy, have not seen eye to eye on this wedding from the beginning. Nicole wants to make a statement, something that illustrates her unique design sensibilities, a calling card for her design firm, which does everything from custom stationery to home goods and furnishings. Aunt Sandy wants everything to be very traditional, old money, old Santa Barbara. Ivory lace and Mexican palms, that sort of thing.

I want whatever makes Nicole happy. She's my closest family member, and probably my best friend, if you don't count Jamie. I feel a little weird about calling a guy my best friend, even if I see him more than I see Nicole.

"Do you think Jamie is going to bring a date to the wedding?" I ask, somewhat out of the blue, even though we are technically talking about the wedding. When are we not these days?

"I'm not sure. Who would he bring? Why, is he seeing someone?"

If he were, I would be the last to know.

"I don't think so. I don't even know why I'm asking. I guess I assumed that since we're both in the wedding party, we could sort of be each other's dates and I wouldn't have to worry about bringing someone for those moments when—" I'm not sure how to articulate it. It's not even something I realized I'd been thinking about. I try again. "Moments when—"

Nicole seems to understand. "Those moments at a wedding when even though you're in a big crowd surrounded by people you don't want to be alone."

"Exactly." I'm grateful there's one person in the world I don't have to spell everything out for. Jamie's pretty good at picking up my vibe, too. But he's not here. He's in L.A. with Ricky, and I'm not going to see him until tonight. My mouth seems to be turned down into a pout. I shake it off. "But that won't work if he brings a date."

"Who cares about Jamie? I definitely think *you* should bring a date, though."

"You do?" I exclaim with over-the-top surprise. She makes a face at my sarcasm.

Nicole has not been subtle with her campaign to see each

one of her four bridesmaids as sickeningly-sweetly-happy, i.e., established in a romantic relationship, as she is. We've had varying levels of success resisting her machinations thus far, but the Never-a-Bride(smaids) group does help.

"I know you don't need me to remind you that I don't date," I say.

"I'm aware," she says flatly. Nicole is convinced that my dating moratorium is more a phase than a lifestyle choice. "We just need to find you a good guy. How about one of the fifteen guys who try to hit on you every time we go to a bar?"

I wrinkle my nose. The surfer bro college students who hang out at the State Street bars are not my type. Not that I have a type. If I did it would be "guy who won't fall in love with me." So far in my twenty-five years I haven't had much luck hitting the winning combination of nice, attractive, and disinterested in a committed long-term relationship.

When I was younger, I had crushes on guys and we'd go on dates and sometimes even have sex, and then they'd want to spend every minute with me and tell me they loved me and I really didn't want all of that emotional stuff. I never felt that deeply about any of the guys who proclaimed to love me.

Is it really so much to ask? Take me out. Date me. Fuck me. But don't fall in love. Don't ask me to marry you and have your babies. Because the answer to that will always be hell no.

Maybe if I had completely changed my personality it would have been possible to turn into some one-night-stand junkie, but it only took me a few attempts at casual sex to realize that shy librarians trying to have flings turn into balls of anxiety, and no one ends up having much fun.

Hence, spinster.

"Come on, O. Let me fix you up. One time. It could be your wedding gift to me!"

"Nic, you sound deranged. I'm not letting you fix me up as

some sort of project. Besides, I don't have a problem if Jamie goes stag to the wedding anyway."

Nicole sighs dramatically. "Fine. But the offer stands. We have six months until the wedding. Plenty of time to find you a nice, hot guy and make Jamie totally jealous."

I practically snap my neck whipping my head up to level a stare at her. "What do you mean, jealous?" The notion that Jamie might be jealous of me having a date to the wedding sends a curious spike of adrenaline through my chest.

"You know, that you've got a date to the wedding and he doesn't. He's barely dated at all since Kara moved to Seattle last year."

"Oh, right. Well, maybe you should fix him up, too." I say it because it's the first thing that occurs to me, but I immediately regret it. If Jamie gets a girlfriend, I won't be able to monopolize his time anymore. And I might have to own up to the fact that being a self-proclaimed spinster can be pretty damn lonely sometimes.

After brunch Nicole goes off to prep for a guest appearance on a design podcast that Kate, who produces them professionally from her home base in Los Angeles, set up. I need an antidote to all the talk about wedding dates, so I message the Never-a-Bride(smaids) thread.

> How are your Sundays going? I need some
> love from my fellow spinsters

KATE

> It's Sunday? I'm at work. The joys of being
> self-employed

ROSIE

> I'm also working but on lunch break. Hospital
> is super busy

LANI

Watch who you call spinster. I refuse to answer
to that until I'm at least 65

> I'm attempting to normalize the term and
> remove the stigma

LANI

How's that going for you?

> It would be going better if I could make
> everyone read my favorite book, Miss
> Rumphius.

ROSIE

The kids book about the girl who becomes a
librarian & plants all those flowers?

> Written & illustrated by Barbara Cooney. First
> published in 1982. Gorgeous pictures. Miss
> Rumphius has three goals in life: to go to
> faraway places, to return home to live beside
> the sea, & finally & most importantly, to do
> something to make the world more beautiful

KATE

Are you a librarian or something?

LANI

Just looked it up. This explains SO MUCH.

> What do you mean?

LANI

You're Miss Rumphius, O! Right down to the
bun! And you already live beside the sea.

> But I've never been anywhere. I need to travel

> And make the world more beautiful

KATE

You will

ROSIE

You have time

> Sometimes it doesn't seem like it. I feel like my
> life is already going by too fast

KATE

I like that Miss Rumphius is a miss—she never
marries, right?

> Never. She's my favorite spinster.

> Once she figures out how to make the world
> more beautiful they call her the Lupine Lady
> for all the lupine seeds she sows

ROSIE

Lupines are lovely

> I adore them

LANI

Should we start calling you Miss Winesap, O?

> Better than That Crazy Old Lady, which is
> another one of her nicknames

LANI

Figures. She sounds ahead of her time, in any
time.

> That's why she's my role model

LANI

Like I said, this explains so much

CHAPTER 5

OPHELIA

I compulsively smooth my hair away from my face while I wait for Jamie to pick me up for our movie outing. I've left my hair long tonight, hanging down my back instead of twisted into my Miss Rumphius-inspired bun. But tonight I don't want to be bothered pinning it up. The unfamiliar softness as it rubs against my shoulders makes me feel like a different person.

I idly flip through one of the wedding magazines Nicole pressed upon me at brunch. The wedding isn't for months, but I can't shake the feeling that I'm already behind schedule.

My gaze snags on a couple posing in their wedding duds in front of a vintage car. The guy looks a little bit like Jamie, only with thinner lips and less dorky glasses; the girl next to him is buxom and short. They look obnoxiously happy and I scoff, shoving away the uncomfortable feeling that it's only a matter of time before Jamie pairs off and gets married to another science nerd, and I'll have to find myself a new best friend.

A horn tap breaks me out of that depressing line of thought and I grab my bag and lock the door of my tiny bungalow behind me. It's not raining now, but I skirt some puddles before throwing myself into Jamie's black hatchback.

Jamie has been known to drive his zippy car to the limits on twisty canyon roads, which I find both exhilarating and an irritating display of machismo, but tonight he navigates the dark, wet city streets cautiously.

"Do you want to get some food?"

I'm not really hungry, but Jamie has the metabolism of a teenager. "Sure. Burgers?"

"You read my mind." We stop at The Habit on State Street, huddling under the canopy with the few other diners. Jamie tells me about his favorite sessions at the maker conference, but after a while he laughs. "Wow you aren't listening to me at all, are you?

"No, I was totally listening." I scramble to recall some keywords from his monologue. "Something something virtual reality voice recognition nanotechnology?"

"Sort of." He grins. "It's okay. Tell me about your weekend."

I flash back to my conversation with Nicole this morning. "It was fine."

He arches an eyebrow at my weak description.

"Hey, Jamie, are you—" I stop. "Do you think—" Huh. This isn't coming out right. "Are you bringing a date to the wedding?" I manage to spit out. I know, I wasn't going to say anything, but all day my brain's been snagged on the idea like a dress on a thorny bush and if I don't just yank, I won't be able to move on.

"Uh. I'm not sure," Jamie says, carefully. "Why?" He takes a bite of his burger and I fiddle with my French fries. I don't even know why I ordered them. I'd rather have a milkshake.

We never talk about this stuff. Dating. Romance. Sex. Especially sex. Mostly because when we first met I was going through a rough patch where Nicole wanted to set me up with every guy she knew in Santa Barbara, and I'd saltily informed Jamie that in order to be my friend we were never to discuss such things. He took me at my word and he's never broken his promise. If he goes on dates, he doesn't tell me about them. And I don't want to know. I've never analyzed exactly why, I'm just relieved that he doesn't seem to need to provide a blow-by-blow of whatever social life he has outside the little universe we share.

Now I'm breaking my own rule. Because the idea of him coming to the wedding with a date churns my stomach enough for me to want to protect myself in some way. Forewarned is forearmed and all that.

"You know Nicole, she wants to see everyone paired off," I start, though it's kind of pathetic to blame this conversation on Nic, as if I'm too much of a wuss to talk to my best guy friend about wedding dates, for goodness sake. Which I sort of am.

Jamie nods, chews, swallows. He looks as if he has no idea where I'm going with this. That makes two of us.

"I thought if you weren't bringing anyone, then we could hang out at the wedding together." I'm so bad at this, it's no wonder we never talk about it. Normally my antisocial behavior doesn't interfere with my friendships. I actually like my friends, so I feel comfortable being my normal antisocial self around them.

"You want to be my date to the wedding?" Jamie sounds extremely confused.

"No! Not your date. You're the best man and I'm the maid of honor and both our families are going to be crawling all over the place and weddings can be kind of stressful and..." I trail off and hope this is one of those times when Jamie understands what I'm trying to say without my having to say it.

"Oh. Well. I hadn't thought about it," he says, again using that careful tone as if I'm a skittish cat he's trying to coax down from a tree.

"Right. I know it's not for a while." I'm never talking about this stuff with him ever again.

"But I think it could be nice if we—" He stops self-consciously, and this is so much worse because Jamie is never self-conscious. He's kind and funny and sometimes a little absentminded-professorish. He makes me feel *normal*, even though I know I'm not.

"I mean." He clears his throat. "I'd be into us hanging out together at the wedding. If you want. We…we could look out for each other, if that's what you mean."

I let out a breath. "Yes, exactly. Look out for each other. Great. That would be great."

He curves his perfect lips into a smile and doesn't quite meet my eyes. "Great."

"You don't mind? Aren't weddings sort of supposed to be, um, fertile hunting grounds?"

"What are you talking about?" He's back to eating and talking with his mouth full.

"You know, the tux, the champagne. If you wanted to bring someone, it's a pretty romantic setting. I wouldn't want to get in the way. Nicole said she could help me find a date, so I don't want you to feel obligated or anything."

My brain isn't certain why my mouth is continuing to speak, especially after he already agreed to what I was hoping for in the first place. But it occurs to me that squiring his friend-cum-cousin around a wedding isn't Jamie's first choice. Maybe he wants to bring a date, a girl he has a chance of actually hooking up with, and I should stay out of the way.

"Are you saying *you* want to bring a date to the wedding?" he asks.

"Me? No, we're talking about you." Why is this so hard? "I'm saying I don't want to stop you if you want to bring a date." Which is mostly true.

"Do you want me to bring a date?"

"I don't care. I want you to do what you want to do."

"Okay."

"Okay."

I have no idea if we've resolved anything, but he seems annoyed enough to leave the last third of his burger uneaten, while I've moved to some new level of awkward that has no name. My unrelenting embarrassment makes my cheeks feel hot, and my previous enthusiasm for our evening shrivels to the size of a raisin.

"If you're done, let's just go."

Maybe the movie will have the magical ability to alter our memories and erase this conversation from our consciousness forever.

He stands up and for a second I think I'm off the hook, but then he says, "So, to be clear, what I want is for us to go to the wedding. Together. No dates."

"Okay," I say, because that's what I want, too. Isn't it?

Something about this entire thing has left me more uncertain than I was before. I shrug, and we go watch superheroes blowing stuff up in the name of saving the world.

CHAPTER 6

JAMIE

I jolt awake a minute before my alarm is set to go off, my brain awash in the details of the extremely erotic dream I was having, my dick hard and leaking. It doesn't take ten strokes and I come with a grunt, before my alarm starts blaring.

The dream wasn't even that graphic, at first just a blur of colors, the sensation of soft, warm flesh. But these dreams, which I have embarrassingly often, are always about Ophelia. Dream Ophelia is always happy to touch me, to be touched. She wears—well, it's a dream, so she doesn't wear much at all, something flimsy and pink that matches the blush in her cheeks. I get to run my hands through her beautiful hair. I get to look and taste and touch my fill—nearly.

After those dreams I always feel vaguely guilty. O doesn't deserve my pointless fantasizing about her. Each time I promise myself it's the last. But then the ache, the want, builds up over days, a few weeks, and my subconscious gets the better of me.

It doesn't matter how hard I try to repress it, I've wanted to kiss Ophelia since the first time we met, over Thanksgiving dinner at Ricky's parents' house. We bonded over a mutual love of pie. I had a girlfriend and I never thought I'd be the kind of guy to hit on someone when he was already in a relationship, but I liked everything about her. If I'd had even the slightest hint that she was interested in me, I would have broken up with Kara that night and begged Ophelia to give me a shot the next day.

But no sooner had we debated pumpkin pie versus pecan and I'd already decided Ophelia would fit just right tucked against my side, she squashed the notion of me ever asking her out. Ophelia didn't do relationships, she informed me. She didn't even want to talk about them with me. I found myself agreeing—I told myself the whole wanting to kiss her thing would pass.

I was wrong.

* * *

Alanna stops by the lab right before lunch. I'm struggling to get the demo set up for a class of third graders I have this afternoon. She looks at me, amused, before she points out I have neglected to plug in the glue gun I'm trying to use to attach googly eyes to the tentacle monster we're making out of found parts.

"You mean you have to plug it in?" I joke weakly. I've been out of it all day, still rattled by O's and my conversation last night.

"You okay, Jamie?"

"Yeah, I'm fine. I'm just—" I set the glue gun down so it can properly heat up. "Can I ask you a hypothetical question?"

"I love hypothetical questions."

"If you have to go to a wedding, and your friend also has to go to that wedding, and neither of you have dates so you agree to go to said wedding together, does that make it a date?"

"I don't know. I don't think it's a date unless you both agree that it is. Otherwise, it's just two friends going together, right?"

I frown. "That makes sense."

"But if you want it to be a date, you should ask."

That's the problem in a nutshell. "I can't."

"Have you dated anyone since Kara? Maybe you need to get back on the horse. Ask her. What's the worst that can happen?"

"I'm not afraid of rejection," I say. "Rejection is guaranteed."

Alanna scrunches up her face in confusion. "If you know it's not a date, why did you think maybe it could be?"

"I don't know, okay? Maybe I'm looking for something that's not there." I'm an idiot. There is no loophole in Ophelia's availability.

Alanna's expression softens. "Weddings can be rough. When my brother got married I drank so much I was still blitzed at the going-away breakfast the next day."

"And this is going to be an intense wedding."

"When is it? Do you need the day off?" Alanna's a stellar manager.

"June 20th."

Her eyes go round. "What? That's in six months. And this girl is locking you in now?"

"So?"

"If she doesn't want to date you, then she should let you at least have a chance to find someone else to go with. Selfish much?"

"She's not selfish. It's complicated." My shoulders slump. "Is it pathetic that even if I don't get to be with her as her date, I'd still rather go with her than anyone else?"

"Not pathetic, Jamie," Alanna says. "She's lucky to have you for a friend. Even if you guys are a little bit codependent. We're talking about Ophelia, right?"

I should have known I was being transparent. I nod.

"Well, I'm not so sure she wouldn't jump at the chance to change your relationship status. I've seen the way she looks at you."

"I don't think so. Ophelia might feel somewhat…proprietary toward me, but she doesn't see me like that."

"Okay, fine." Alanna shrugs and fakes nonchalance. "Do what you want. Be a coward."

I definitely regret bringing this up with the most stubborn member of The Fox staff. "I'm not being a coward," I grit out. "I'm respecting her wishes." Flouting the carefully agreed-to terms of our friendship is bound to lead to one or the other of us ending up hurt. And since hurting Ophelia is the last thing I'd ever want to do, I'd probably end up bearing the hurt myself in order to protect her.

"Yeah, you're right, a girl who asks her guy friend to go to a wedding six months in advance is totally not into said friend." She crosses her arms and gives me a pointed look. "You know, I thought you were smart, but I've been wrong before."

"Hey, I resent that. You don't know Ophelia like I do."

"That's my point, Jamie. No one knows her like you do. And trust me, she wouldn't want it any other way."

* * *

My mind's only half on work the rest of the day. I'm not convinced that Alanna's right, but the ambiguity of it all has me feeling off-kilter. Ophelia's contradictions are one of the things I like about her, but they're also bewildering.

Ophelia isn't like anyone else. She's jaded about the traditional but endearingly enthusiastic about stuff she really cares about, like vintage enamel pins and doughnuts. She's bookish and quiet except when she lets loose her dry sense of humor. She's beautiful but cares less about how she looks and more about making her environments cozy and touchable, from her storybook cottage of a house to the library she runs with drill sergeant precision and a generous spirit.

And she's different when you get her one on one. I get it, I'm the same way. The constant flow of people through the museum is exhausting, so after hours I want to hang out with a few good friends and have real conversations. When it's just Ophelia and me we can relax and be ourselves. That must be why it feels so good to be with her.

On the other hand, I spend a fraction of every minute we hang out reminding myself that we're just friends and that's all we're ever going to be. I need a break from the emotional gymnastics, otherwise it's going to be a long six months.

CHAPTER 7

OPHELIA

"I don't understand why you're having a Super Bowl party. No one here cares about football." I don't bother to disguise my crabbiness as I deposit my offerings on the bar that separates Nicole's kitchen and sunken living room. The pregame show plays on the big flat screen hanging across from the brown leather sectional, but thankfully the sound is muted.

"Honey, it doesn't matter if we don't care about football—it's practically a national holiday. Thanks for bringing guacamole, by the way. It looks delish. La Croix?" Nicole holds up a can of my favorite soft beverage—grapefruit flavor all the way. That, plus the flattery, makes me feel a little better.

I take the drink and overload a tortilla chip with guac. I shrug off my jacket and flop down on the couch with a sigh. I don't have a specific reason for being in a bad mood, but I've been out of sorts for a week. I haven't seen Jamie since the night we went to the movies. Not that there's a connection.

"What's eating you?" Ricky asks as he bounds into the room. He's always reminded me of a Dalmatian puppy—serious, eager to please, and full of energy for doing the right thing. He lives his life ready to come to the rescue, should it be necessary. Not that Ricky's a firefighter. He's a venture capitalist whose only hobby besides making money seems to be doing whatever Nicole wants him to. No one can dispute that they are utterly devoted to one another, but he's way too shiny for me. I'm happy for Nicole and happier still that I don't have to wake up next to a Ricky every morning.

"Nothing. I just don't understand why everyone gets so worked up over watching a four-hour football game."

"I watch it for the commercials," Ricky says.

"You could watch those on YouTube."

"She's grumpy because it's been raining all week," Nicole says, carrying a platter of enough food to feed both football teams, even though I'm pretty sure that besides Jamie and me they only invited a handful of other people.

"Why would that make you grumpy? I thought you loved rain."

I'm surprised Ricky remembers that. I always had the impression he barely registered me.

"I do love rain, thank you very much, and I'm not grumpy." I realize I say this in a cross tone, but I can't take it back. I sigh again. "I just don't like football." It's a lame excuse for my mood, but the real reason is even lamer, so I go with it. Nicole eyes me like she knows something's up, but she leaves it alone.

It's not long before Rosie arrives with her boyfriend, Gus. They've been dating since the fall, but they're already planning to move in together, house hunting every weekend for a new place down the road in Ventura. This is ironic because not long ago the four of us bridesmaids, Rosie, Lani, Kate, and me, swore we'd never walk down an aisle, unless at the request of someone wearing white.

Nicole is well-meaning, but she thinks everyone needs to be paired off like penguins. The four of us were decidedly against marriage, for ourselves, at least, if not the institution entirely. I don't trust it, but live and let live.

Rosie betrayed the cause and is now deliriously happy to be

one half of a couple. I don't begrudge her happiness. I like Rosie, even if at first I found her a little intimidating. She's wicked smart, a doctor, and classically pretty. Gus looks at her like she's personally responsible for making the sun rise and set, and worships her accordingly. It's sweet, if sometimes nauseating.

"Hey, Ophelia." Gus takes a seat on the couch across the big coffee table from me and starts piling a plate with food. "You rooting for the home team or are you a traitor like Rosie?"

I give him what I assume is a blank look.

He tries again. "The game? Who do you want to win? Rosie has decided the underdog should win even though their quarterback is a scrub."

"I don't like to see the same team win over and over again," Rosie says, plopping down on the couch next to him. "It's boring. Plus, the scrub is cute."

"Oh, you think he's cute, do you?" Gus tickles Rosie in the ribs. She giggles and bats his hand away in a very un-doctorly way.

"Yes," she says, "objectively. Though he's really not my type."

"And what is your type, hermosa?" Gus grins at her wolfishly and she blushes.

Apparently, their relationship is in a highly flirty stage. God, just what I need—to be around more couples.

I like my solo life. I should have left well enough alone and not brought up the wedding date thing with Jamie, because I keep replaying that excruciating conversation in detail and it's made my week not fun, to say the least. I have a tendency to torture myself with any embarrassing slipup for years. My brain helpfully cues up my greatest hits when I'm trying to fall asleep at night.

Why is it so embarrassing to talk about this stuff with Jamie anyway? It's not like he cares if I date or not. He's too nice to tell me to stay out of his business. The Kendell men are all *nice*. But Jamie's nice in a different way. He's nice to people he likes—smart people, interesting people. Which is not to say that he's a snob, intellectual or otherwise. He doesn't care what kind of education you have or what your background is. If you want to learn, he'll teach you. But he doesn't bother making nice to people just to make himself look good. I appreciate that. He's genuine. You know when he smiles at you, he means it.

That makes me feel...I don't know. Good, I guess. Like I matter. He always makes me feel like I matter to him. That's something I hadn't had in a long time before we started hanging out. And it's something, if I'm honest with myself, that I've come to rely on.

Gus and Rosie are ribbing each other about the football game and who has the better chance of winning. Gus's hand is on Rosie's knee and his thumb circles over her kneecap in a casual intimacy that I can't seem to tear my eyes away from. My bad temper is creeping back in, so I chug half my sparkling water and let out an involuntary burp.

"Nice to see you, too," Jamie says, materializing on the couch next to me as I blurt out, "Excuse me!" It's definitely not the first time he's seen me humiliate myself, but my cheeks warm a little bit anyway.

"Uh, hi." I lean forward and set my drink on the table. Gus, Rosie practically sitting in his lap, plants a sweet, but intentional, kiss on her lips. I shake my head, uncertain why I care so much about some minor PDA. I'm happy for Rosie. She's a sweetheart. Just because she's clearly bailed on our seriously unserious non-marriage club doesn't mean I don't want her to be happy.

What is with me lately? I suppose Nicole's wedding fever has caught me, too, thinking about my life choices and wondering if I've been missing out on something by standing so firmly in the no-relationships camp.

Since casual sex is definitely not my thing, and sex with someone I care about inevitably leads to them wanting more from me than I want to give, the solution has been to become a very young old woman. I've inverted maiden-mother-crone. Nothing wrong with that. I know how to take care of my own physical needs, which isn't as boring and clinical as it sounds. And there are lots of people who aren't interested in having sex with other people. It's an absolutely valid life choice.

It's just that sometimes I feel like I've put myself in a box and I'm too stubborn to admit that the box's hard edges don't always have to be so rigid.

I'm not lonely. I have friends. I have Jamie. Who is right this minute sitting six inches away, paying more attention to his phone than to me. His hair is a little damp, and I can smell him, woodsy and clean. He must have recently showered. Which means he probably went for a run earlier, since the rain has finally broken. For some reason thinking about Jamie going for a run and getting all sweaty, then taking a shower right before coming to the party makes me feel a little squirmy.

He bailed on our lunch dates this week, and he hasn't talked to me since he sat down. A little voice in my head reminds me that if he's being weird it's because I fucked up by breaking our no-talking-about-relationships rule.

I stand abruptly, drawing eyes as I stalk back to the kitchen.

"I'm going to go home," I say as Nicole dumps a bag of chips into a wooden bowl. "And for the love of God, stop putting out food. There are six people here. Six!"

"Like hell you're going home," Nicole says pleasantly. "You're going out there and visiting with our friends and having fun if I have to handcuff you to the sofa."

"That might liven things up a little," I say sulkily.

"Come on, the game's starting in a minute. Ricky's got yummy stuff on the grill and I know you haven't seen Jamie all week. Why don't you guys catch up? Here, give him this for me." She hands me a beer, Jamie's favorite bottled brand. Not his favorite draft. Is it weird that I know the minutiae of his beer preferences?

"Give me two." I might as well get over myself and have some fun with the remainder of my weekend. I stomp back to the couch.

"Here." I thrust one bottle at Jamie and open mine with the stylish bottle opener Nicole, the consummate hostess, placed on the coffee table. I drink the first half as rapidly as I consumed my sparkling water, and my stomach rebels at all the fizz.

"How was your week, Jamie?" I ask, taking a stab at normalcy.

"Fine, Ophelia, how was yours?"

He still hasn't looked up from his phone, so I poke him in the side. "Rainy. Are you betting on the game or something?"

"Huh?"

"What are you doing on your phone?" If I sound like I'm complaining, it's because I am.

"Oh, sorry. Had an idea on the way over. Trying to get it down." He taps at the screen a little longer, then puts it away. He meets my gaze and instantly the knot inside me loosens, his attention soothing my ruffled feathers and calming my anxiety.

He's brilliant, I know, and I forgive him his phone time. He often has crazy ideas, little tweaks to his systems, his lab, his designs, ideas for his programs at the museum, things that might pan out or might bomb spectacularly. He keeps an open mind about them all. I admire him so much, and I'm reminded of a favor he did for me this week.

"Hey, thanks for sending me the link to that online design software. Jewel's been using it to get her California mission project done."

"She's the one you told me about?"

"Yeah, she loves the maker lab so much. I think she might

be a good candidate for STEAM camp at the museum, if we can find her a scholarship."

"I'm sure we can work something out."

Suddenly, the force of his smile, crooked and genuine, makes me self-conscious. I drain the second half of my beer as the game starts and we have to listen to the droning announcers try to make an extremely stupid game exciting. But Rosie's not wrong—both quarterbacks are awfully good-looking. With my beer goggles on, I start to have fun.

By halftime, I'm feeling pretty loose, cruising on my second beer, laughing and joking with Rosie and Nicole while the guys pretend to be knowledgeable about the plays and stats and whatnot. The hamburger and copious snacks have slowed my buzz. I debate and decide I can have one more drink.

When I collapse back down on the couch, I end up halving the distance between Jamie and me. I can definitely smell him. He smells good. He doesn't seem to be paying any more attention to me than he is anyone else in the room, and that annoys me, just a little. I jump to my feet with the vague idea that I'll trade my beer for water—and two things happen simultaneously.

I snag my sandal's heel on the rug, lose my balance, and have the presence of mind to notice that I am falling straight toward a bowl of salsa, so I pitch myself sideways in midair. But my foot, the one that caught and started this whole mess, is stuck, so everything goes sideways except for it. There's a popping noise, and I find myself crumpled in an undignified heap at the end of the couch, pain searing up my leg starting in the general region of my right pinky toe.

Well, shit.

CHAPTER 8

JAMIE

One minute Ophelia is passing in front of me and the next she's on the floor between the couch and the oversized, heavy wooden coffee table with dangerously sharp edges. I throw myself down next to her, running my hands over her head, smoothing away wisps of her hair.

"Did you hit your head?"

"No, it's my foot," she says, trying to sit up, but wincing as she extracts her sandal-clad foot from beneath the coffee table.

There's no blood, but I can see her right pinky toe is red, maybe swelling up. I help her onto the couch. Her face is paler than usual.

"Let me see," Rosie says. I remember that Rosie is a doctor, and I move over sheepishly. What little medical knowledge I have is from middle school sleep-away camp. The protocol for poison oak or snakebites is not applicable here.

"Why does a stubbed toe hurt so much?" O asks, with less than her standard level of irritation. That worries me.

"It's not stubbed, it's dislocated," Rosie says calmly.

"Gross!" Nicole sticks out her tongue.

I glare at her. "Should we take her to urgent care?"

"I can take care of it, if you want." Rosie is looking at Ophelia. Obviously, she's the patient. Maybe I'm overreacting.

I order myself to put some distance between us and let go of O's hand, which I realize I'm clutching. Or is she clutching me? But I can't bring myself to let go, so I stay put, and O holds my hand tighter as Rosie efficiently strips off her shoe.

"Breathe, O." Rosie pops the toe back in with a barely audible snap.

"Fuck!" O says, but she seems to be feeling a bit better now that one of her bones is no longer out of its socket.

"You're going to ice it, and you might want to take something for the pain. You need to stay off it for a few days." Rosie's in full-on doctor mode, calm and reassuring. She's making me feel better, anyway.

"A few days! I have to work."

"You can go to work but try to sit and keep it elevated."

"Sure, easy," Ophelia says sarcastically. "I know librarians have a reputation for sitting behind a desk all day, but believe me, that's not what I do."

"So let Ingrid do the running around and you can catch up on your computer work," I say.

"I guess I can do that." She looks lost. Her mouth is pinched. The sight of her in pain is doing weird things to my heart. I feel like I've run a mile flat out.

"I'll go get you some ice." Of course, to do that, I have to stop holding her hand. She meets my gaze, her eyes wide. I give her a nod and let go.

Nicole's in the kitchen with an ice pack already wrapped in a towel. She gives me a lopsided smile. Is that pity I detect in her eyes?

"What?" I say curtly.

"Nothing."

"You're being weirdly chill about this."

"She's fine. You've got the worrying covered."

I don't dignify that with a response and hurry back to Ophelia's side.

She's still sitting on the floor, and she's washing down a pill with my bottle of Stella.

I swipe the bottle with my free hand. "Take it easy, O." Carefully, I wrap the flexible cold pack around her injured foot.

"Hey, that's medicinal," she says.

"Jamie's right. You don't want to mix what I gave you with alcohol. It's pretty heavy-duty. I only happen to have it left over from some dental work I had done."

"Oops," O says, then giggles. She sounds loopy already.

"I'll drive you home," I say.

"How will I get to work tomorrow?"

"Maybe you should take a sick day."

"Nonsense. I'll call Ingrid to pick me up in the morning."

"And I'll get you after work. Ricky can bring your car over tomorrow."

Negotiations complete, Ricky and I settle O into the passenger seat of my GTI. She looks small and frail, her injured foot propped on the dash. I ignore the stretch of bare leg she's showing as her skirt rides up her thigh.

"Take care of her," Nicole demands, but mildly.

"Call me if you need anything. She'll be fine in a few days," Rosie says soothingly. I must look upset or something. I thank everyone and make our escape.

It's a fifteen-minute drive from Nicole and Ricky's place by the Mission to O's on the south side of town.

"It's a good thing you dislocated your toe so we didn't have to watch the rest of the game," I say, trying for a joke.

"Why did you go if you don't like football?"

The honest answer is that I knew she was going to be there, so of course I wanted to be there, too, but what I say is, "Nicole seemed jazzed about the party."

"There were six people there. And football is the world's

most boring game. Sport. Whatever." She leans her head against the window and sighs. "I feel funny."

"Your toe? Does it hurt?"

"Not anymore. Whatever Rosie gave me was the good stuff. I feel a little…floaty. Fuzzy."

"I don't like seeing you—" I stop. I've had to monitor myself more lately. I'm in the danger zone and I need to be careful.

"Is that why you skipped our lunches this week? You don't like seeing me anymore?" She sounds strange, a little drunk, actually.

"No, that's not what I meant. I don't like seeing you in pain. I skipped our lunches because of the rain." And because sometimes hiding what I feel for her is harder to bear.

"Stupid rain." She's looking out the window, and I almost don't catch it when she says, "I missed you."

Then we're at her house. I eye the twenty feet between the curb and her door and make a split-second decision to pick her up and carry her. She's a soft bundle of curves, but I focus on the task at hand and not on how good it feels to hold her. She doesn't protest, or say anything at all, except for a quiet "Thanks," when we get to our destination. I carefully set her down on her good foot. She stares at her front door as if she's never seen it before.

"O? The key?"

"Right. I'm a little dizzy." She leans on me, and I force down a wave of panic. I've only seen her drunk a handful of times. This is worse. She's almost disoriented. I know, rationally, that she'll be okay after a good night's sleep, but I can't stop the apprehension from growing inside me.

"I got it." I try to sound relaxed while I fish out my own key. I've carried one ever since she locked herself out twice in a week last year. Of course, she hasn't needed it since then. I use it for the first time, and the lock opens smoothly.

I elbow open the door and propel her straight toward her

bedroom. Her place isn't much more than an open kitchen/living room and a bedroom and bathroom. Hardly bigger than a studio, but she has it decorated with touchable fabrics and bright, cheerful colors, poppy red and turquoise and sunflower yellow.

I sit her down on the side of the bed while I pull down the covers. It's a strangely intimate action, one that has the devil on my shoulder wishing I were pulling down the crisp sheets for us to crawl under together.

I banish the thought and help her lie down with her head on a pillow.

"James?"

I pause in the act of sliding off her remaining shoe. I vaguely wonder what happened to the other one. Nicole has it safe and sound, no doubt.

"Yeah?"

"You smell good."

I ignore the zing of awareness her words send through me. She smells good, too, like sugar and lemons. She must be super out of it on whatever Rosie gave her. "You need to sleep this off."

"Sleep, sleep, sleep," she sings. Yeah, she's zonked. "Sleep with me."

"Absolutely not." That's an easy one. No way will I subject myself to that kind of torture.

But then she grabs my hand, or tries to, kind of flailing around, and I glance at her face and she looks really...young. My protective instinct kicks in with an unwelcome jolt. What if she needs something in the night? What if she has a bad reaction to the medicine, something worse than just being silly? What if she wakes up in pain and can't walk and—

I'm not sure if I'm doing it for her, or to assuage my own fears, but I nod. She smiles, then closes her eyes. "Sleepy."

"Yeah, I'll bet." It's barely eight o'clock. I figure I can stay with her for a while, then move to the couch for the remainder of the night. I set her phone down on the nightstand and plug it in so it'll be charged for her in the morning. The clothes she's wearing look comfortable enough, so I'm spared the agony of figuring out how to get her into pajamas with my sanity intact.

I slip off my sneakers and remove the ice pack from her foot. Her toe looks pink and a little swollen but not too bad. I have no idea what side of the double bed she sleeps on, but I push her farther over to the right so her injured foot can stick out of the covers. Then I settle myself on her left and turn off the light.

"I'll be here if you need anything," I whisper, though I'm pretty sure she's already asleep.

No such luck.

"I know," she says. "You're always there."

I don't know why her words depress me so much. Actually, I do know. Because I am always *here*. And she's always *there*. And she's never going to be there for me the way I want to be there for her, if that makes any sense. I'm starting to feel a little punchy, too.

"James, Jamie, James. I like both. Jamie is the museum guy who's good with kids. James is the inventor with the secret patents and the kissable lips."

Wait. What?

I've never seen Ophelia kiss anyone. She isn't into kissing anyone. But that's what she said. Kissable. Lips. Mine. Maybe she means it in an objective 'Jamie has kissable lips if you're into that sort of thing, which I am not' way. That makes sense.

I lick my lips, suddenly hyper-aware of them.

Unless she means mine are specifically kissable. Possibly by her.

The potential of that has my stomach jumping on a trampoline. If she thinks my lips are kissable, then maybe it's not wrong for me to think her lips are kissable. Maybe all my ruthlessly suppressed attraction doesn't have to be so ruthlessly suppressed. Maybe the best woman I know might sometimes think of me as more than a friend or cousin-in-law. Maybe that's something I can work with.

Or maybe I'm a dope who's doomed to wanting someone he can never have.

Either way.

I close my eyes for what feels like a second, but when I open them again the blurry numbers of her alarm clock show it's close to midnight.

I hear a noise and realize that what woke me was Ophelia, moaning a little.

"O, are you okay?"

"Mmm. My toe hurts."

"Where's your ibuprofen?"

"Drawer."

It's dark, so with my phone screen lighting the way I open the bedside table drawer. Inside is indeed a bottle of over-the-counter pain meds. There is also a tube of lube, an egg-shaped vibrator, and two different-sized hot pink dildos.

I stare at them for a long minute. Am I hallucinating? Maybe this is a dream. Or maybe I'm just invading her privacy. I grab the bottle and shut the drawer.

She takes the pills I hand her. Either she's still high from before or too sleepy to care that the drawer she sent me into also contains sex toys. Or she doesn't care that I see them. How much more evidence do I need that she sees me as only a friend?

I hear her settle back down. I roll over, but it's a long time before I return to sleep.

CHAPTER 9

OPHELIA

I *didn't drink enough to feel this much like shit.*

It's Monday morning, and as I attempt to sit up in bed the night before flies back into my brain in about ten seconds. Most of it, anyway—the football party, falling, the pop as Rosie fixed my poor toe, Jamie driving me home.

Jamie—I'm alone, but I distinctly recall him being a solid, warm presence for most of the night. I had been really out of it, but I remember I asked him to stay and he stayed.

He's nowhere to be seen now. I don't feel like dragging myself out of bed quite yet. My toe doesn't hurt too badly. The hardest part about recuperating will be staying off it long enough for it to heal properly. My head, however—blech.

I reach across my bed for my stash of ibuprofen and another detail of last night pops up. Asking Jamie for these pills. Hearing him go into this drawer for them. It was dark. Maybe he didn't notice the dildos?

A girl can dream, right?

I'm currently too woozy to be embarrassed. Jamie would never judge me. And he's too much of a guy to even bring it up. So we won't say anything. Just like we don't say anything else about sex, or dating, or romance. That's our rule, after all. Even though I broke it myself only last week, I went through enough angst to have learned my lesson.

I push aside thoughts of loyal friends, sex toys, and dislocated toes, and focus on getting myself to work. My phone is charged—likely thanks to Jamie. I text Ingrid, who agrees to give me a ride to school. I shower and dress and microwave some leftover steel-cut oatmeal for breakfast. While I eat and make sure I have my workbag stocked with what I need, I notice a note on the back of the front door. "Chiefs won! Take it easy today. J."

I have no idea what he's talking about. What Chiefs? But I find myself tucking the note into my planner, a memento of the ill-fated evening and the night I spent with Jamie Kendell in my bed.

* * *

Even though I knew he'd be there, it's still jarring to see Jamie waiting for me in the teachers parking lot when I emerge from the school library that afternoon.

He's leaning against the hood of his car, wearing his museum shirt and a gray hoodie in a nod to the weather. He's not on his phone, for once, but reading an actual book. Reflexively, I note the edition of the Neil Gaiman paperback.

I take a moment to simply appreciate the sight of an attractive man reading a book. He's a repressed librarian's wet dream, lanky and lean, rectangular glasses and square jaw, long fingers, dark fringe of hair. He looks up, sees me, and the world kind of stops for a minute. I watch him watching me. It shouldn't matter—it doesn't matter, I tell myself—that his mouth quirks up into a secret sort of smile. I want to believe it's the smile a friend gives another friend casually, but I know better.

It's the smile a friend gives to his friend when he's discovered said friend has a stash of sex toys.

Fuck.

I walk slowly to the car. My toe isn't bothering me that much. I'll ice it when I get home and ensconce myself on the couch. We don't talk as he opens the passenger door for me. He takes my bag so I can settle myself inside, then hands it back to me.

We ride in silence for a while. Then he says, "How was your day?"

Are we going to pretend? Is that what I want? I decide to play along.

"A bit inconvenient to stay off my feet, but not too bad. Ingrid is a saint."

"She'd have to be."

"What is that supposed to mean?"

"Putting up with four hundred elementary kids every day. Not to mention you."

I know he's teasing. "You deal with kids every day, too."

"In smaller doses."

"Anyway, I feel okay. And thanks."

"For?"

"For last night," I say. But that sounds wrong. I don't want him to think about how I asked him to stay over and sleep in my bed and medicate me and...something niggles at the back of my mind. Did I do anything else embarrassing? I'd probably remember. Right?

"You know, helping me get home and everything." I try to sound nonchalant.

"I was happy to," he says. He doesn't elaborate, but I get the feeling he's thinking about something in particular. The sex toys?

"I was pretty out of it," I say. It's both an apology and a subtle plea for information.

"The stuff Rosie gave you was pretty strong. Not to mention you're five foot nothing so it probably affected you more."

I hadn't thought of that when I was washing the pill down with beer. "You're right. I shouldn't have taken anything. It didn't hurt that bad."

"And now?"

"It's fine! You don't need to take care of me." My words come out sharply, and I instantly feel bad. He's been nothing but helpful and sweet. I owe him a favor—or dinner at the very least. "I'm sorry."

"It's okay," he says, but I think we're both relieved when he pulls up to my little house.

"Let me buy you dinner, to say thank you. We can order sushi and watch *Harry Potter and the Prisoner of Azkaban* again." It's our favorite of the film adaptations. A mindless night of sushi and a movie with my best friend sounds like heaven. I love living alone, but sometimes it gets lonely, just me and my houseplants and my books. I get weary of being strong, single Ophelia all the time.

"Uh, I can't." He looks vaguely guilty and I can't stop my brain from going somewhere it shouldn't. Does he have a date? My stomach grows queasy.

"All right." I ignore the pang of disappointment. "Soon?"

"Yeah, definitely. Sounds good."

I open the door, anxious to get away from him. He knows I need help, even if I don't want it. He's out of the car in a flash, helping me again with my bag and the door and making sure I'm settled inside.

"See ya, O." I watch from my front window as he drives away, oddly sad for no good reason.

* * *

Later that night, after frozen Trader Joe's curry instead of sushi and an episode of a reality singing competition instead of Harry Potter, I lie in bed, eyes wide open in the dark. The harder I try to fall asleep, the more restless I get. I know what to do to relax, but the prospect of using my toys isn't appealing. Damn Jamie. I did not need that complication. Our relationship has skirted into strange enough territory lately.

I skip the toys and use my hands instead, old-school style. I touch myself, lightly at first, soothing strokes on my breasts, my stomach, between my legs, feeling the familiar comforting rush of endorphins. I haven't had sex with anyone in a few years, but I've gotten really good at self-pleasure. A spinster still wants to come.

I have a rotating line of guest stars in my fantasies. The usual hot geeks get their turn. But tonight, no matter how hard I concentrate on imagining Benedict Cumberbatch using his cupid's bow mouth between my legs, he keeps slipping away to be replaced with Jamie—Jamie's mouth, Jamie's hands.

It's not like I haven't thought about Jamie that way before. He's attractive. It's a fantasy, for goodness sake. But lately, thinking about him is more complicated than simply getting myself off to the most convenient daydream.

Because Jamie's not a fantasy guy—he's within arm's reach nearly every day. His eyes, flashing at me with amusement, exasperation, worry. His lips, curved up in that deadly smile, or flattened in disapproval, or pursed around a bite of something sweet and sticky and...this isn't helping. Actually, it is helping me get closer to my unusually elusive orgasm, but it feels wrong. Unfair to him, and a bad idea, and the naughtiness is kind of a turn-on and I'm closer and closer, pressing against myself harder and harder, faster and faster, until the pressure builds and crests and then pops like a champagne cork.

I cry out and float down on the fizz of the champagne bubbles spreading through my body. I'm sated, relaxed, ready for sleep, and I sternly tell my mind to turn off and save thinking about the implications of masturbating to my best friend for another day.

CHAPTER 10

JAMIE

"I have to talk to someone about this and unfortunately I don't have anyone else."

"Gee, thanks." Nicole isn't really mad. In fact, she's vibrating with excitement that I asked her out to lunch, just the two of us. She can smell gossip a mile away. Not that I don't trust her. If I tell her something in confidence, she'll keep it that way.

The trouble is, I'm not exactly sure what I need help with. I've been confused since the night Ophelia asked me about wedding dates and everything that's happened since then has made me more mixed up.

When O asked me to stay for dinner last night, all I could think about was that we would be sitting together on her couch, laughing, eating, and it would be so, so easy to just stop her between bites of spicy tuna roll and kiss her. I wouldn't be able to take it back and everything would be different and—my mind had overheated with all the millions of possible outcomes, most of them terrible. It was easier to evade and tell her I was busy.

But I can't spend the rest of my life avoiding the woman

who's become my best friend. Since Nicole knows Ophelia better than anyone, I thought I'd get some advice.

"So what did you want to talk about?" Nicole asks after we order and find seats in the crowded outdoor patio. There's a chill in the air, but it's too beautiful a day not to sit outside. Nicole looks warm enough in her faux-fur coat, anyway.

"Uh, right. It's sort of hard to explain." So much for gaining clarity.

"Is this about Ophelia?" Trust Nicole to be blunt.

"What do you think?"

I'm expecting a simple yes, but what I get is, "I think you're in love with her and you want to know if I think you have a chance."

I choke on my iced tea. "Jesus. I don't know if I'd put it like that."

Love? I'm a few steps away from calling whatever there is between me and O *love*. I mean, sure, in the sense that I love my close friends and family, I love Ophelia, too. But having for so long thought there was no possibility of her ever reciprocating my feelings, being in love with her is something I've denied myself the pleasure, and the pain, of considering.

"How would you put it? You're not giving me anything to work with here, Jamie."

She's right. I'm being a chickenshit.

"You know O and I are close," I start. Nicole nods and gestures her impatience. "Like best friend close."

"I'm her best friend, but yeah, I know what you mean."

"A few days ago something happened and it got me thinking that maybe O is interested in sexual relationships. And maybe she's even interested in...me?" I refuse to dwell on the dildos and focus more on the "kissable lips" thing.

"And this is bad?"

"Yes! No." I take a breath. "It's bad if it changes things. You know I want to stay in her life. She's important to me."

"Sex always changes things," Nicole says with a shrug. "That's a cliché for a reason."

"Fuck." Something else occurs to me. "Wait—if you knew I had feelings for her, I must be fucking transparent as hell. Does she know? Does she think I'm a crazy stalker or something?"

"Calm down. Ophelia's not the most observant person when it comes to emotions. That's why she's so bad at relationships. The only reason I said anything was because I know you haven't dated anyone since Kara and I see the way you look at O, and I figured, even if you didn't know, you're stuck on my cousin. Which I think is sweet. But—"

"But?"

"Look, Jamie." Nicole's tone softens, and I fear we're dangerously close to pity territory. "Ophelia is complicated. Her parents' divorce did a number on her. Most girls crave commitment and she runs from it. And you, poor bastard, may be her best guy friend and she might think you're more than passably attractive with the absentminded-professor-with-a-six-pack shtick you have going on, but she knows, deep down, you're built for serious monogamy. For a girl who's idea of hell is falling in love, that's the most dangerous kind of guy."

She pats my arm consolingly. "Which means you, cousin, are out of luck."

The truth of her words hits me like a ton of Lego bricks and I hope I don't look half as crushed as I feel.

"It's too bad, though. If I ever thought she'd take the plunge, I'd wish she'd do it with someone like you."

If my world weren't imploding right now, I'd be touched.

"Thanks." It's not like I didn't sense what I'm up against on some level. But hearing Nicole put it all out there is rough.

"Now eat your burger and cheer up. There are lots of fish in the sea."

"That's a cliché, too," I mumble.

"Like I said, for a reason. Look, there's one right now." She points her fork toward a pretty black-haired woman on the other side of the patio. I can't muster even passing enthusiasm. Because the more I think about how off-limits Ophelia is, the more I want her. It's completely perverted and beyond stupid. But she's the only woman I can think of.

Could I change her mind? Or could I change myself into someone who can be physically intimate with the woman of my dreams and not get involved emotionally?

Ha. She'd stomp all over me.

Might be worth it, though. If after things inevitably fall apart we could go back to just being friends, if we could still meet for lunch and joke and talk. Of course, if things go really sour, we'd still have to contend with seeing each other at every Winesap-Kendell family gathering for the next fifty years.

My thoughts must be playing out on my face, because Nicole says, "It's not a good idea, Jamie."

"I get that," I snap, my anger at the situation finally getting to me. I have to decide. Do I accept what we have—a deep and abiding friendship—or do I try for something more and damn the consequences?

"So your advice is let this thing with Ophelia go and date other people?"

"Basically."

"I don't want to date anyone else." I know that with bone-deep certainty.

"You're going to pine for her the rest of your life?"

It's not an appealing prospect. What we have isn't bad. But it was much easier to endure when I didn't know she was inter-ested in my lips and...*sex toys*. I'm a guy, okay? I'm visual. And the visual of her lube, vibrator, and other goodies is never going to be erased from my lizard brain.

Since I'm fresh out of ideas and Nicole is no help, finally I make a noncommittal gesture and paste a fake smile on my face.

"So, what's up with you?" I ask my cousin-to-be.

Nicole has no problem moving on from the train wreck of my love life and launches into a diatribe about the latest cummerbund fiasco or something equally mind-numbing.

I'm grateful for whatever blunts the pain of realizing I've somehow gotten my heart broken by someone I've never even kissed.

CHAPTER 11

OPHELIA

* * *

Nicole may be high-handed about it, but I know the drill. When the universe hands you an unseasonably warm Sunday in February, you go to the beach.

I throw a novel into my bag, along with my SPF 100 and my

straw hat. I score a mostly legal parking spot two blocks from the beach and head toward the sand. I see Nicole first, in a saffron-colored polka-dot caftan. She's set up a pop-up tent, Lizzo blasting on her portable speakers.

"Where's Ricky?" I ask.

"Some guys asked them to play volleyball a little ways down the beach." She gestures south. I shade my eyes and pick out the volleyball net and two figures on either side.

"Them?"

"Ricky and Jamie."

"Oh." Of course Jamie is here.

"Problem?"

"No!" Why would it be a problem? Just because he's been a little weird lately. Or am I the one who's been weird?

"I brought sandwich stuff."

I glance down at our picnic blanket and the feast that Nicole has set up for four people. It looks like she bought out the entire deli section of Whole Foods. "I can see that."

"Want to go tell the guys food's ready?"

"Sure." I leave my stuff, kicking off my sandals. My toe feels so much better, only twinging for a second as I start across the sand barefoot. It feels like we've all been randomly time-traveled to the height of summer. I'm wearing a bikini, but I don't intend to get any sun on my skin unless it's through a thick layer of sunblock, so I keep on my peasant blouse and cut-offs.

Ricky and Jamie have their backs to me as I approach the volleyball game. I watch as the other two guys, short, muscular twentysomethings with close-cropped black hair and prominent upper arm tattoos, serve it up. Ricky looks like a walking J. Crew ad in his trunks and polo shirt, exertion tinting his white skin strawberry red. But he can play, and he returns the serve. The other side gets it back over the net, and Jamie spikes it over, just out of reach of the other player.

Their opponents swear good-naturedly and toss the ball

under the net. I can't take my eyes off Jamie as he preps his serve. His dark hair is extra curly in the heat, his angular glasses seem out of place, but his thigh muscles bunch and flex exceedingly nicely under his medium-length trunks. His back muscles ripple as he sends the ball zinging over the net in one fluid motion.

I can't remember the last time I saw him without a shirt on. Maybe last summer? And I don't remember him being quite so...chiseled. Is that the word I'm looking for? Every one of his muscles is defined. I had no idea that his museum uniform has been covering up a flat, ribbed stomach, long, muscular arms, pecs that have an intriguing hollow running between them, flat brown nipples. He has his mother's olive skin, rather than his dad's Irish pastiness, and here it's on display in all its Mediterranean glory.

I swallow, belatedly realizing he and Ricky have notched another point and are serving again. There's no harm in watching, I tell myself, even though I can't seem to take in anything except Jamie and the way his muscles move as he sprints over the sand.

Jamie is hot as fuck.

The thought intrudes on my mind, unwelcome but indisputable. I have the strongest urge to run over to him, push him down on the sand, straddle him. I want to feel all of those muscles for myself.

I shiver. I have goose bumps and it's eighty-five degrees.

"Hey, O," Ricky calls, pulling me from my unwanted fantasy.

"Hey," I choke out. I clear my throat. "Uh, Nicole says lunch is ready."

"Game point," Jamie says. "We'll be over in a minute."

"'Kay." I should turn around now and scrub the vision of Jamie playing beach volleyball shirtless from my mind forever. But I have a feeling the image isn't going anywhere.

Maybe something to that effect shows in my expression because Jamie's smiling at me oddly. He's too busy looking at me to see Ricky's setup and he loses the point, which at least wipes the smirk off his face.

I don't stay to watch the end of the game after that. I've seen enough.

On my way back to our spot, my phone pings.

ANDY WINESAP

Free for lunch?

A familiar mix of irritation, guilt, and affection washes over me when I read my dad's text. Considering we live about a mile away from each other, we don't see each other much. In fact, Jamie probably sees my dad more than I do. They're both members of an informal breakfast club of geeks and design nerds that meets Saturday mornings at a greasy spoon by the railroad tracks.

I should tell him to come by and partake of Nicole's picnic, since he spends half his life at the beach anyway, painting watercolors for tourists.

Sorry, can't. Soon? ☺

We never regained the closeness we had when I was a kid, when our family made sense, my parents and me making a tidy triangle. Things were simpler then.

My parents ran their own graphic design company out of our house. They were a team. Mom was the business-oriented one. Dad often said that without her, he'd be painting beach scenes for tourists and living on pasta. I didn't realize for a long time that though he always said it as a joke, a part of him wished that's the way his life had gone.

A few weeks after my fifteenth birthday they dropped the bomb. They were getting a divorce.

I suppose I was stuck in teenage myopia because I didn't see it coming. Oh, I knew my mom looked a little more brittle, was a little more snappish with my dad, and Dad was spending more weekends camping with his friends than at home with Mom and me. But I was shocked when I found out they'd been talking about separating for almost a year. The happy little unit of three I thought we'd been was suddenly broken.

Dad moved out, taking his books and his art. They dissolved the business. He rented a little shack down by the beach, too tiny for me to stay over. Living his dream, I thought bitterly.

Mom left Santa Barbara the minute I went to college, moved to Malibu, and took a corporate job in a shiny skyscraper. But it's the loss of closeness with my dad that I haven't really been able to get over. Mom and I never had much in common, but she's easy enough to get along with. I'm proud of her for reinventing herself, and I'm glad she's happier now.

It seems like the person who got the rawest deal in the Winesap divorce was me.

"What's wrong?" Nicole asks when I finally make it back to the tent and start assembling a plate for lunch.

"Nothing. Dad texted me."

"Oh." My dad is Nicole's uncle, and since she's five years older than me, she's known him that much longer. She knows he means well, but communication isn't our forte. "How is he?"

"I don't know. Good, I guess."

"And how's your mom?"

"Fine. I haven't seen her since Christmas." I don't want to talk about my parents, and how the distance between us seems to grow with each passing year. I'm close as can be with my cousin, but it's not the same thing as having a real family to belong to. I realize that if I stick to my Miss Rumphius-inspired plan, I will indeed become an old lady who entertains the neighborhood kids and her great-niece, Nicole's grand-daughter.

If I'm lucky.

This is the only life I'm going to get. I glance behind me as Ricky and Jamie saunter toward us. They're what constitute my family these days. I can't let them go or I'll have no one. I can't mess things up with Jamie by being inconveniently attracted to him.

And then Jamie, his curls weighed down by sweat, his T-shirt slung over his sculpted shoulder, smiles at me. "Hey, Ophelia."

My stomach clenches and I feel suddenly oxygen-deprived. "H-hey."

What the hell am I going to do?

CHAPTER 12

JAMIE

After the beach, I'm a mess, sweat and sunscreen gluing sand to my skin. I need a shower. A cold one, thanks to hours of proximity to Ophelia and her bikini.

Instead I head straight to my workshop. Maybe I can get out some of my frustration through hard work.

I converted my garage to a workshop about five years ago—about when I started getting into welding and my kitchen was always in danger of catching on fire. I've been tinkering with my new printer design. I need to get the prototype finished so I can move on to some other projects. I grab goggles and gloves from my tool rack, but hesitate before diving in.

Normally I start messing around with my gadgets and hours will fly by as I lose myself in solving problems. Somehow I get into the zone and at the end something new has been created. It's a heady feeling—knowing I'm contributing to the world. It makes me feel alive. But today I stare at my tools and materials without really seeing them.

All I can see is Ophelia, and a version of my life in which she's more than my friend. One where she's my partner in all things. I'm not an expert on women, but I can tell when someone's attracted to me. And ever since the night she called my lips kissable, believe me, I've been looking for a sign that she meant it.

The way she looked at me while I was playing volleyball was unmistakable. She looked like she was stranded on a desert island and I was the last can of La Croix. The rest of the day she treated me with an underlying snappishness. No one's that snippy with someone who's just a friend.

Is this a problem I can engineer my way out of, or are human emotions too complicated for the engineer's approach? Design and build a working robot? No problem. Convince one incredible woman to give me a chance? Impossible.

My gaze settles on the one living thing in my shop. It's a fern, flourishing in a plain terra-cotta pot. Ophelia gave it to me for Christmas, along with strict instructions on how to keep it alive. It still looks healthy, green and bright among the gears and gadgets. She worries that I don't get enough fresh air when I spend so much time in my workshop. Not sure the carbon dioxide-oxygen exchange from one houseplant is going to improve things much, but it's pretty to look at.

Suddenly, my perspective shifts. Ophelia is already embedded in my life, as I am in hers. She cares about me, even if she's never said as much. I can't let myself not even try.

What if I approach it like an engineering problem? If I can play to my strengths, so much the better. I need all the advantages I can get. Because a woman is way more complicated than a robot.

The first thing I teach my classes of makers when they are approaching an engineering or design problem—say, the ideal beach umbrella—is to define the problem. Okay, let's go.

Problem defined: I want my best friend. I need her. I'm crazy about her. I'm totally up for meeting her for lunch, going to the bar, seeing a movie, exactly like we do now. I'd just like to be able to kiss her hello at lunch, to wrap my arm around her at the bar to let all the yahoos who are thinking about hitting on her know she's not available, and to hold her hand at the movies, then go back to our place and make passionate love over and over again until we wear ourselves out.

And she doesn't.

Or at least she doesn't want to admit she does, because her parents fucked her up good and proper with their messy divorce.

That's a pretty big problem.

Next, I tell my students to imagine a solution to their problem. This involves imagination, vision. How would their ideal beach umbrella look? Would it have anchors to keep it from blowing away in the wind? Would it have built-in cupholders for their small-batch kombucha? Would it have a sunscreen dispenser or a Bluetooth speaker system? Often this stage involves drawing a picture.

I remove my goggles and gloves and grab a piece of graph paper and a pencil.

Hesitantly, I sketch one of my most basic fantasies involving Ophelia. We're at Nicole and Ricky's wedding. She's the maid of honor. I'm the best man. We're dressed to the nines. I sketch myself in a suit, make myself recognizable by the messy hair and rectangular glasses. Ophelia is next to me, in a frothy squiggle signifying a fancy gown. I've drawn her heart-shaped face, lips pursed as if she's about to kiss the cartoon me, our hands linked.

We're there together, not simply as members of the wedding party or family of the bride and groom. We're there because we've chosen each other. We dance all the dances and we try to make each other laugh inappropriately when the toasts go on too long, and when it's all over and Nicole and Ricky are on their honeymoon and we all have our lives to ourselves again, we go home together. Because that's what we are now. Together. Always.

This feels hopeless. I'm about to crumple my stupid sketch and toss it in the recycle bin, but I don't let my students give up on their designs midway through. If their ideas are too out there, they can refine. Not give up.

I'm not giving up.

Third step: make a plan of action. I have to woo her without scaring her off. I resolve to do one thing every day to advance myself from miserable pining to becoming the wedding date of the woman of my dreams.

It doesn't matter how long it takes. I can be patient. I have the ability to hyper focus on a problem until it's solved. I have a large body of knowledge about Ophelia's likes and dislikes. I can use all of this to make myself as appealing as possible.

All it takes is for her to let go of her fears and insecurities long enough to see that maybe we'd be perfect together. I'll focus my efforts on transitioning our relationship from the platonic-friend zone to the possibly non-platonic.

If it doesn't work, I'm no worse off than before, and maybe I'll finally be able to move on.

Here's hoping I won't have to.

CHAPTER 13

OPHELIA

I wait at our bench, squinting at a sun so bright it makes the Pacific a few hundred yards away gleam like polished silver. Jamie arrives out of breath, as if he's run the two blocks from the museum. As if he's in a hurry—a hurry to see me?

It seems like he's going to kiss me hello, the way his parents are always kissing acquaintances as if they're French or something, so I tilt my head, trying to give him my cheek but he goes for the other side and his mouth ends up grazing mine. I pull away sharply.

"Sorry," he says casually. "Hey."

"Hey," I manage. Why is everything between us so tense lately? It bugs the hell out of me that I'm overanalyzing every tiny thing.

"I brought you something," he announces, which is when I notice that in addition to his lunch bag he has a small brown box, the kind that usually holds sugary yummy things.

"Give it," I demand.

"After you eat your lunch."

"Yes, Daddy," I say with mock sweetness. I can't help but hear the kinky undertones of the remark and immediately wish

I hadn't said it. Jamie doesn't seem to notice, just sets the box down out of my reach and starts eating his lunch.

I take out my food and start with flavored yogurt, the least healthy part of my meal, to spite him.

"How many oceans have you seen?" I ask.

"Two. Atlantic. Pacific. You?"

"One." I gesture toward the nearest available ocean.

"At least it's the best," he says.

"Is it? How do you know?"

"It's got Hawaii. And Fiji. And Bali. And Alaska."

"Have you been to those places?"

"Only Hawaii and Alaska. But I know I'd like the others. I like to be warm. I like green things."

"Me too," I agree. Not that what he's saying is so groundbreaking. Who doesn't like warm, tropical places? "I like being by the water. I've never been to an island."

"Not even the Channel Islands?"

"No."

"My dad took me camping on Anacapa once. Sort of felt like what it might have been like here hundreds of years ago."

"Like *Island of the Blue Dolphins*."

"Exactly."

"One of my favorites. It still makes me cry."

"Doesn't every book make you cry, though?" He's teasing me, but he's not completely wrong, so I swat him on the arm.

"Whatever. Don't tell me you didn't get choked up when Dumbledore died." Jamie read all seven Harry Potter books at my insistence, finishing the last one a few weeks ago.

"It was worse when Fred died. Poor George!"

"Stop! Or you'll get me started, too." I wipe at the sympathetic tear that springs to my eye.

"Yes, no need to rehash the tragedies of Harry Potter. Don't you think he and Hermione should have gotten together?"

"Yuck, no. Hermione and Ron are perfect for each other.

Not that I think every character needs to end up paired off by the end of a book."

"Of course you don't."

"What does that mean?"

"You're enlightened." His voice is nonchalant. "You don't think people need to be in a couple to be happy. And you're right."

"I sense a but coming on."

"*But* being in a couple can be nice."

"Yeah, everything is rainbows and unicorns until you wake up one morning and realize the person you thought you loved is actually the worst."

"How would you know?" He asks it so softly, it shouldn't feel like a dagger just slid through my heart, but it does.

When I don't answer he says, "Have you ever been in love?"

This question alarms me for multiple reasons. One, the last time we talked about relationships, I was out of sorts for a week. Two, is he trying to tell me something? Is he seeing someone? Three, I don't actually know how to answer the question. I loved certain things about people that I've dated. But in love? I guess if I have to think about it this long, the answer is, "No. I don't want to be."

"Why not?"

"Why are we talking about this? Do you—are you dating someone?" Why is the question so hard to spit out?

"What? No." He sounds almost incredulous, which doesn't make any sense.

I do the thing I do when I'm uncomfortable and want to get out of the spotlight—turn it on someone else. "Have *you* ever been in love?" I ask, feeling like this conversation is completely out of my control and I'm an idiot because there's something going on beneath the surface but I have no idea what it is.

"Yeah, I've been in love."

"Kara?"

"If I had loved Kara, wouldn't I have gone with her when she moved?"

"I don't know. Why didn't you go with her?" At the time, I had been so happy that Jamie wasn't moving away and I'd get more time with him to myself that I didn't overanalyze the reasons for the split.

"I wasn't in love with her," he says dryly, as if it's obvious.

I hate feeling like I'm missing something.

"Oh." Must have been some other girl, before Kara. Before I met him.

"And the reason we're talking about love—isn't it traditional?"

"What are you talking about?"

He hands me the brown box. Nestled inside is a single vanilla cupcake with chocolate icing. Tiny pink sugar hearts stud the top.

It's Valentine's Day. Duh.

"I forgot." I shoot him a rueful grin. "But thanks for this."

"You're welcome."

"You didn't get one for you?" Jamie's sweet tooth rivals my own.

"Nah."

"We can share it." I quickly shed the treat of its paper case and hold it up for Jamie to claim the first bite. It's the least I can do for being a dick about Valentine's Day and a Scrooge about love. He glances at me, then at the cupcake.

"All right." He lowers his head, takes an enormous bite and beams at me with chocolate on his lips, his mouth full.

I should be outraged at his effrontery, but I'm too mesmerized by the frosting coating his top lip and too shocked by the intense desire I have to lick it cleanly and thoroughly off.

I watch helplessly as he swallows, then uses his own tongue to do the job, which is almost more erotic. I can imagine him doing other things with that soft, pink tongue, exploring my mouth, mapping a trail down my body, licking a stripe over my pussy, tonguing my clit until I come.

Uh. Danger, Will Robinson. I'm way too far down the rabbit hole and he's staring at me like I'm about three feet over the red line that establishes the boundaries of our relationship.

I stuff my mouth with a good portion of the cupcake's remains so I don't have to talk. "Thanks," I mutter around a mouthful. "Gotta get back." I gather my stuff and run like the coward I am.

CHAPTER 14

OPHELIA

E ven though I live in one of the most beautiful places in the world, I've always longed to see certain other parts with my own eyes. Such as everywhere. I planned to save my pennies, retire early, and take an open-ended around-the-world trip. Very Miss Rumphius. But ever since Nicole and Ricky got engaged, I've been thinking, why wait? Once they're married, next will be parenthood and fulfilling all the rest of their obnoxiously traditional dreams.

Nicole can navigate newlywed status without me. God knows my parents would barely notice if I left the country. And maybe if I wasn't around Jamie all the time, I'd forget about the way he looks when playing beach volleyball. By the time I came home, maybe we'd be able to pick up where we left off—friends without the distracting underlying one-sided attraction.

I push open the doors of The Fox, wave to Alanna, and head for the administrative offices. I'm not here to see *him*. I'm here to pick up a letter of recommendation, the last piece of my application for a librarian international exchange program. I haven't told anyone about it because it seems like such a long shot. They only award five a year, and they get hundreds of applicants.

I tell myself I don't really want it anyway, but it would be pretty fabulous. I'd get to spend a year in another country, learning about their libraries and technology and sharing my approach with them. Library science is just that—a science. There's an order and method to it that can be replicated, but it can also be refined and improved, and different librarians apply it in different ways. Plus, there are differences between libraries for children, teens, and adults, not to mention different types of materials and providing access for all communities to those materials and technologies. But I'm getting carried away. This is the kind of thing librarians can geek out about, and the kind of thing I'd get to really dive into and explore if I got accepted to the program.

Hence, the application. The maker lab Jamie helped me install in my library has been a huge success, if I do say so myself. The CEO of the museum agreed to write me a recommendation based on our collaboration. Mihret Fatuma is a progressive educator, and she sees the museum as an evolving organism that should be designed to provide education to everyone who walks through its doors. We see eye to eye on a lot of things. Which is why when she asks me to sit down across from her in matching sustainable bamboo armchairs and gives me a stern look, I get a little worried. Does she not want to give me the recommendation?

"What's going on?" I ask.

"I think this exchange program sounds superb, Ophelia, and after they read the glowing recommendation I'm giving you, they'd be crazy not to accept you," she says. "But I'd be lying if I said I thought it was a good fit for you."

"What? Why?"

"No one knows the needs of local children better than you. You have so much important institutional knowledge. Why not stay here and expand on the programs we already have in place?"

"What do you mean? I've sort of tapped out the resources at my school. I can write grants until I get carpal tunnel, but there's a limit to the resources one school can absorb."

"Why not think bigger? We had such success with your ideas. Why not expand them to the entire district? I've located some money in the museum's budget, and I know three private partners right off the bat who wouldn't blink at donating to cover the rest. You could spearhead it, get a nice stipend."

"Wait—are you talking about bringing maker labs to more schools?"

"To *every* school, K through 12, district-wide. I'd loan you museum staff. Jamie Kendell could advise on the tech side. You'd be doing the high-level stuff, and you and Jamie could develop a curriculum to train the teachers and librarians who would be managing their own labs. If we work on the proposal now, we could start installing labs in the fall. What do you say?"

"You're seriously saying we have the funding for this? And offering me a job?" The idea of bringing maker labs to more schools has been rattling around in my brain, but I had no idea how to make it a reality. Mihret is offering me a chance to make a massive difference in the education of thousands of kids.

"Yes and yes. If you get this fellowship, I can probably find someone else to lead this initiative, but there's no one who knows what we're trying to accomplish with these labs better than you. This would be a huge step for you, too, Ophelia. If you ever wanted to leave Clinton and come over to the museum world, this kind of thing would really give you a leg up."

My head is spinning. Her offer is so tempting. It would bring innovation to the city on a much larger scale, a way to make a difference for every child, not only the few hundred at my school.

"I have to think about it," I say. It sounds like a wonderful opportunity, but I'm not ready to make such a big commitment at the drop of a hat.

"Of course. I'll email you my ideas in more detail tonight, and I'll loop Jamie in. Maybe the two of you can sit down together and send me back your notes next week. We can move forward from there."

"All right. Thank you, Mihret."

She smiles warmly. "I understand why you want to travel, Ophelia. After college, I spent three years filling up the pages of my passport before grad school. But right now, I think you're needed here, where you can make such a difference. The world will wait for you."

I'm a bit preoccupied as I leave her office, so I'm not prepared when another door opens right in front of me, and I pull up short.

"Sorry!" It's Jamie, dressed in his museum clothes, a half-eaten apple in one hand. The rest appears to be in his mouth. He chews quickly. I must be staring at his mouth because he swipes over it with the back of his hand.

"Shit, did I mess up our lunch day?" he asks. "I have a class coming in fifteen."

"No, I have to get back to school, too. I had a meeting with Mihret." This isn't the time to elaborate. "I'll tell you about it later."

"Dinner? I'll bring something over."

"Sounds great, but only dinner. No dessert."

"What?" He looks genuinely shocked and I laugh.

"The wedding may be months away, but Nicole has very strongly hinted that I should be able to fit into my bridesmaid dress now, then, and forever."

"Don't listen to her. You'd look great in a paper bag. She's going to micromanage you to death."

"It's her big day."

"Yeah, day. Not year. She doesn't get to boss everyone around indefinitely." He sounds like he has personal experience with Nicole's bossing, and I narrow my eyes.

"Why? What does she have you doing?"

"I don't want to talk about it."

There seem to be a lot of off-limits subjects for us lately. "So, see you later?"

"I'll be there. I can't promise there won't be gelato. It's up to you if you're going to have some or not."

"Evil wretch," I mutter. It seems I have a lot to digest tonight.

CHAPTER 15

JAMIE

"Three pints, really?" Ophelia says when she sees what I've brought. Three flavors of gelato, plus Thai takeout.

"Brain food. I thought we could talk about Mihret's idea for expanding the maker lab program. She filled me in on your meeting before I left."

"Right. We should talk about that." She gets out plates and I dish out hot, fragrant noodles, rice, and veggies. I stick the gelato in the freezer.

I was anxious to get to Ophelia's and talk about Mihret's proposal. I simply want to be near her, to hear about her day and tell her about mine, and possibly also gauge how successful my oh-so-subtle campaign to get her to see me as something beyond platonic BFF is going.

We have spent as much time together as we usually do, but she seems jumpy, as if she's holding something back. Since I'm always holding back around her, I understand the feeling.

Maybe that jumpiness means things are changing. If she's even half as attracted to me as I am to her, we're both suffering from unresolved sexual tension. One of these days, we're going to be strung so tight from keeping our hands off each other, something is going to snap. I only hope it snaps us together, not further apart.

I have no intention of pressuring her, but eventually I'm going to have to make my intentions clear. If I don't actually say anything, I'll always wonder what-if.

"So let's talk," Ophelia says, as we settle into our usual spots on the couch with our plates.

I know she doesn't mean talk about us, but part of me wants to go there anyway. I school myself. Not yet.

"I think it's a terrific idea. We always said that the lab at your school was a pilot program, but I didn't think they'd get the funding sorted out so quickly."

"Me either. It's certainly what I'd hoped would happen. I guess I didn't envision Mihret choosing me to lead the initiative. I thought Clinton would be a model and I could give my input, but someone else would expand the program."

"You'd be perfect for it, though. We learned so much installing your lab. What works, what doesn't. Now we have the usage data for the kids at your school and we have the case studies of how the teachers are integrating the lab into the curriculum. It's awesome."

"It would be pretty amazing to design a training program for all the librarians and teachers, to make sure they'll get the most out of it. You can advise on the tech side, make sure we get the proper hardware, software. It would be a lot of fun."

"So you're going to do it?" I'm excited about the idea of working with her again. Setting up the maker lab together was incredibly satisfying. She's detail-oriented and knows her students so well. She anticipated which features they'd use and which they wouldn't, and she taught me a lot about the needs of the students and how the lab could support them and inspire them.

She chews her noodles thoughtfully. "I'm definitely interested. I think I'll go ahead and tell Mihret I will work on the formal plan. But I have to tell you, I may not be here to implement it in the fall."

I freeze with a forkful of noodles halfway to my mouth. "What do you mean?"

"I've applied for a librarian exchange fellowship. I sent in the application today, actually." She sounds matter-of-fact, but she's avoiding my eyes.

"Oh. What kind of exchange?"

"I'd be assigned to a library in one of twenty countries, all room and board paid for, to work there, learning about all the local innovations, the latest technology. I'd be on sabbatical from my job, and when I came back I'd bring back so much more knowledge."

"When you come back?"

"Yeah, it's a yearlong program."

"Wow. It sounds—" *far away* "—like an incredible opportunity."

"It's really competitive," she says. "So I probably won't get it."

"They'd be lucky to have you. When do you find out?"

"Couple of months, I think. So, if we start this program and I get the fellowship, Mihret would have to find someone to take over for me."

"Oh. I'm sure she could find someone." But it wouldn't be the same. Ophelia has always dreamed of traveling. I know she wants to see more than our tiny, if beautiful, corner of the world. But she always talked about it like a long-term goal. Not something she was actively pursuing. I guess I thought I had more time. That we had more time. Because how could they take one look at her application and not accept her? She's remarkable.

Suddenly, my appetite is gone and I fiddle with my glasses. The smile I give her feels funny on my face. "Good luck, O. You deserve an opportunity like that."

"Thanks," she says softly.

The atmosphere should be celebratory, so many exciting things happening, but I'm oddly deflated. "Let's break out that gelato," I say, trying to change the vibe.

"Right." O seems to shake off a mood, too. "S'mores, green tea, or huckleberry?"

"What do you think?"

"Some of each?"

"Yes, please."

A few minutes later we're back on the couch, bowls of gelato in our laps. I don't give Ophelia any shit about her generous portion. I fully intend to warn Nicole against giving O any complexes about her bridesmaid dress and her figure. She's perfect the way she is.

O's telling me about some of the fourth grade mission projects when I get a flash of inspiration. If she ends up leaving for an entire year in a few months, I don't have time to waste warming her up to the idea of us as a couple. I need to pull out the big guns.

"Let's watch a movie," I suggest.

"Really?" She wakes up her phone to check the time. "We have to work tomorrow."

"Yeah, but tomorrow's Friday. Do you always have to get your eight hours?"

"I guess not."

"Besides, with the sugar in the gelato, we'll be up for a while," I say. "If we go to bed now, we'll just be lying there, staring up at the ceiling. Nothing to do." I deliberately phrase my words so she'll be thinking about beds, and me, and how to possibly fill any sugar-stimulated hours.

She gives me a weird look. "Sugar doesn't usually keep me up."

Jesus, she's stubborn. "Fine, we'll start the movie and if you get really tired, you can go to bed."

"What do you want to watch?"

I pretend to deliberate. "I've been meaning to see *Don't Look Now*. I think it's streaming somewhere."

"*Don't Look Now*? The old horror movie with Donald Sutherland?"

"And Julie Christie," I confirm.

"Isn't that the one—" she stops, and I see a hint of a blush on her cheeks.

"The one what?" I prompt. I know what she's thinking. There's an urban legend that the lengthy sex scene between Donald Sutherland and Julie Christie was real. Kind of gross, or kind of sexy, depending on what you're into.

"Isn't that one too scary, though? Right before bed?" I know she's reaching. I shake my head at the image of her leaping into my arms during the scary parts. We're not in high school. But the fact that she seems embarrassed to watch it with me is good. It means that she'd feel uncomfortable watching a sexy movie with me, possibly because of where both of our minds would inevitably lead.

"You're probably right," I say. "How about *The Sandlot*?"

"And now for something completely different," she jokes.

"Or we could play truth or dare," I offer.

"What? What's with you tonight?"

"I'm bored," I say. "And I'm hyped up on gelato. Let's do something." I lean toward her a little. Her eyes widen.

"Something?"

I lick my lips. "Got any ideas?"

"Um."

I wait. She usually has zingier comebacks than "um." Better and better. Slowly, I lift my last spoonful of huckleberry gelato to my mouth and take a bite. I feel idiotic, as if seduction by ice cream ever worked for anyone. But still, she's watching me, watching my mouth, and something thrums between us, something unspoken but so real it practically has a pulse of its own.

If kissing could be done telepathically, I swear we'd have our tongues down each other's throats by now. I'm clenched so tight I'm practically quivering.

She laughs sharply, sits back, and the thrumming thing between us disappears. "You're putting me on right now, aren't you?"

"What?"

"Is this because of the sex toys?"

"What sex toys?" I ask in a tone that makes it clear I know exactly what sex toys.

"I remember enough about that night to remember asking you for pills which happened to be in the same drawer as some of my toys."

My mind trips on the word "some." Were those the tip of a sex toys iceberg?

"Okay, yeah, I remember seeing some stuff in your drawer. So?" I realize it's a little late to be playing dumb, but the change in her demeanor has me all mixed up.

"Guys are so predictable. They think sex toys equals slutty. You've been teasing me all night, haven't you?" Now she seems hurt, and I feel defensive, guilty, and disappointed all in one cold rush.

"No! First of all—" I stop, not sure which landmine to blow myself up on first, since there are so many at hand. Fuck. "I'm definitely not teasing you. I'm sorry for making you think so. Second, I have never once thought of you and the word 'slutty' in the same sentence. Except maybe, 'Wow, Ophelia is sure not slutty.' And third, I might have been a little surprised by what I saw in your drawer that night, but believe me, I don't think less of you for it. If anything, I think it's super cool." She rolls her eyes. "That sounds lame, but you know what I mean."

My attempt to undo the damage wrought by my pathetic flirtation seems to work a little, because Ophelia doesn't look quite so pissed off.

"So all this, the movie and truth or dare—that was what?"

Of course she's calling my bluff. And I'm not quite ready to show her my full hand.

"Ophelia…" My chest is full of conflicting feelings. I'm going to bungle this. I have to try. "Don't you ever wonder what it would be like?"

"Um."

I pick up her hand with mine. It's delicate and warm. "What *we'd* be like?"

"I try not to," she says shakily, and the sheer hope that her words arouse in me is enormous.

"Believe me, so do I." I hold her hand lightly, not asking for anything more. "But I can't seem to help it."

She doesn't say anything.

"Should I tell you what I think it might be like?" I ask, low and careful.

I watch her internally debate with herself. Her gaze flicks back and forth to where our hands are joined, to my eyes, to some spot over my left shoulder.

"Maybe…later." She looks down, as if ashamed of her cowardice. I think she's magnificent. I'll take that maybe later and keep it close to me.

"All right." I gently remove my hand from hers. "You let me know when you're ready."

I get up and bring our gelato bowls the four feet to the kitchen sink and rinse them out. I pick up my workbag and check my pocket for my phone. Ophelia hasn't moved from her perch on the couch. I want to cross over to her and drop a kiss on her soft hair, but I'm terrified of losing the tiny bit of ground I've gained tonight.

"Goodnight, Ophelia."

"Goodnight, Jamie." She doesn't sound worried, or afraid, or upset. She sounds a little bit happy. My chest is brimming with hope all the way home.

CHAPTER 16

OPHELIA

I 'm way too wired to sleep. It's not the gelato. It's the fucking bomb Jamie dropped in the middle of me in a huff with him about the sex toys thing. I need to process this so I text Nicole to call me.

My phone rings barely a minute later. "Are you okay, honey?"

"Yeah, sorry for bothering you."

"Not bothering me. I'm finishing up a little work."

I forget sometimes that Nicole's not only about wedding stuff. She actually has a job. She's a kick-ass creative person and business owner, but she's never too busy to talk to me. I experience a wave of affection that makes me close my eyes and want to cry for some irrational reason.

"It's about—" Suddenly, I'm scared to keep going. So far the feelings I've been having for Jamie have been something I could tell myself were all in my head. But if I name them, they might be real. I might have to do something about them. I'm not sure if I'm ready for that.

But this is Nicole, practically my sister. And I need her help. "Jamie came over and we were talking and things got—weird?"

"Why? What did he do?" She sounds suspicious, which

confirms my sense that she kind of knows what I'm going to say.

"He didn't do anything. Not really. What did you think he might do?"

"Nothing." She's not a great liar. Clearly she knows something is going on. But I keep the conversation nonconfrontational, for now.

"He said some things that led me to believe that, like, maybe he..." This is way harder to say than it should be, especially considering I'm twenty five and not fifteen. "...wants me?"

"He's a fool."

"Oh. Thanks?"

"Oh, honey, not because he shouldn't want you. Who wouldn't? It's just that he knows you don't do relationships. He shouldn't be making you feel uncomfortable."

I think about the things he's said and done lately. She's right, they have made me uncomfortable. But not in the you're-being-skeevy-leave-me-alone sense. More in the I'm-attracted-to-everything-you-do-and-say-and-you're-making-me-want-you-all-the-time sense. Which is more difficult to explain.

Perhaps my silence speaks for itself because Nic gasps.

"Are you saying you want him to want you?"

This is the part I'm not good at. Actually owning up to my feelings. "I don't know." That's a lie, but Nicole gives it to me as an out.

"You know what, we can fix this. I already told him to forget about having any chance with you because he's the last guy in the world you'd ever date. But in a nice way."

"What? You guys talked about this? When?"

"A few weeks ago."

"And you didn't tell me?"

"He requested confidentiality."

"You told him I would never go for it?"

"Basically." She sounds a little guilty, but it's not really her fault. Before I can reassure her, she adds, "Are you saying you'd consider it? Dating him?" The disbelief-slash-enthusiasm of seeing me in a romantic relationship with anyone is evident in her voice.

"Don't get too excited, Nic." I'd have to get over my innate terror of commitment before I let myself go there. "Wait a minute, if you told him he had no chance, why has he been flirting with me for weeks?"

"I guess he decided not to give up."

"He is very stubborn."

"He's also crazy about you—and don't let that freak you out. Bask for a moment in the knowledge that someone adorable, brilliant, kind, and very good with his hands likes you."

I let her words sink in. It does feel good to be wanted. The way Jamie looked at me on the couch earlier, the way his attention was entirely on me, felt very good indeed.

I could easily be hyperventilating right now at the implosion of one of my most cherished relationships. Instead, I feel a certain amount of relief knowing that the cloud of longing and confusion hovering over our interactions is not one-sided.

"O, you aren't freaking out over there, are you? Do you need me to come over?"

"No. I'm not freaking out. It's just—we're such good friends," I say helplessly. "And we're family. Extended, non-blood family," I clarify, even though she already knows what I mean. "And work is a little complex right now." I still think that fellowship would be life-changing, but working with the museum, with Jamie in particular, to expand the maker lab program also excites me. I'm torn in two directions, and I don't want my feelings for Jamie to factor into my career choices.

"Things are changing. You and Ricky are going to be married soon and then you'll be having babies. And lately, Jamie's sort of become all I can think about. It's weird, and hot, and I don't want to hurt him, and I don't want to get hurt."

Nicole makes a noise meant to comfort me on the other end of the line.

"What am I going to do?" I sound sad, as if failure is already inevitable. "Because I have to do *something*. This is not going to go away on its own. I can kill it, and we can try to move past it. Or we can, I don't know, get it out of our systems? That's a thing, right?"

"Honey. I don't think so," Nicole says gently.

"I know." 'Getting it out of our systems' is a rationalization for doing something monumentally stupid and ends up with hurt feelings all around. Or worse, you never get out of each other's systems and end up staying together. Until one day everything falls apart.

"You can ignore it. Or you can go for it."

"Why do I feel like either way I'm going to lose?"

"Stop thinking about winning and losing," Nicole says impatiently. "Forget about Jamie. Think about what you want."

I think about Jamie on the couch, about him cradling my hand in his. About how that simple gesture made me feel excited, safe, happy, and terrified all at once. I think about how I usually have to read other people's words to experience those emotions, and how someday I want to be brave enough to step into the world and experience things for myself.

"I want him," I whisper. "I want to know what it would be like to be with him."

"So find out."

CHAPTER 17

OPHELIA

OPHELIA

Are you going to N & R's Oscar party this Sunday?

JAMES KENDELL

I was thinking about it. You?

Do you honestly think Nicole would let me get away with not showing?

Fair point. Want me to keep you company?

If you want

I want

...

I have a class coming in. Talk later.

* * *

OPHELIA

We should schedule a meeting to talk about the maker lab expansion

JAMES KENDELL

I'll email you my availability

Thx

* * *

JAMES KENDELL

Ricky just told me the Oscar party is dressy 🙁

OPHELIA

You'll survive. You must have a non-flannel button-down somewhere in your closet.

Ouch. I think I can find something.

Your mom would probably take you shopping if you asked her nicely.

Double ouch

What are you wearing?

To the party, I mean 😊

Not sure. A dress, I guess. Maybe I'll go full ball gown.

Looking forward to it

…

* * *

OPHELIA

Still up?

James Kendell

Yeah

So remember last night?

Yes

It's later

…

Are you sure?

I think so

But

Let me get this out there first. I don't think either of us wants to ruin our friendship. So could we at least lie and say whatever happens, we'll still be friends?

Because I would never trade what we have for a few minutes of…fun

Believe me, O, if we do this, what we'd share would be more than a few minutes. I could spend an hour on your earlobe alone.

…

Oh

I don't want to ruin our friendship, either, but there is one thing I would trade it for

What's that?

More

More?

More touching

More kissing

More tasting

More everything

I think you should call me

"Hey." Jamie's voice is low. I'm lying on my bed in the dark and I can't believe we're doing this.

"Hey. So, I'm probably going to fuck this up." There's a frantic note to my voice that makes me cringe.

"It's okay." Jamie is calm, soothing. I try to breathe. "We're not going to do anything you don't want to do."

I know he means that he's not going to pressure me, that I'm in control, but that kind of freaks me out. It means I'm the one who might go too far. This is big, too colossal for me to get a handle on. Still, I don't want to turn back. I want to see where this thing will lead.

I want to see if I'm going to like it as much as I think I will.

"Can I ask you something?"

"Of course."

"When did this...attraction...start? I mean, when did you know?"

He hums. "Honestly? Pretty much the first time we met."

"What! But you had a girlfriend."

"I was dating someone, but I wasn't blind. I thought you were beautiful. And then we got to be friends and I pushed it to the background. Like, Ophelia's got brown eyes and likes pie and is incredibly beautiful. Just a simple fact about you. No big deal."

I've got a huge grin on my face. He's such a dork. But the fact that he's saying these things makes me feel warm and happy, like Christmas morning. "So you thought I was—" for some reason it's hard to say the word "—beautiful, but it didn't go beyond that, right?"

"I can't say that." I hear him sigh through the phone. "Look, it's not like when I was with Kara I was thinking about you all the time. But when she decided to go to Seattle, I knew that leaving Santa Barbara wasn't what I wanted. Replacing Kara with someone new wasn't what I wanted. Why would I, when I had you in my life?"

I swallow. Kara moved over a year ago, so he's had these feelings for a while. I'm terrified, but also flattered, not going to lie.

"What about you?" he asks.

I know what he's asking but I dread answering.

"Uh, honestly, I've thought about you—physically—for a while. But it seriously never occurred to me that you might see me that way until I asked you about wedding dates. I think I subconsciously realized that if you didn't care about me, you'd be much more motivated to find a date to the wedding."

"Brilliant deduction."

"Thanks."

"And what do you mean by you thought about me physically?"

"You know what I mean." God, I'm such a baby.

"Ophelia." His tone, commanding yet amused, sends a shiver through me. It's a good thing we're doing this over the phone or I would have thrown myself at him three times over by now.

"I think you're cute, obviously. I like your dorky glasses. And your floppy hair."

"And?"

"Ugh. And your stupidly beautiful mouth and idiotically graceful hands, okay?"

"Okay." I can hear his smile. I want to wipe it off his face with my tongue, but he's not here, so I use the only weapon at my disposal.

"I used to think about your hands sometimes, if I lost

interest in a movie we were watching together. I'd imagine you putting your hand between my legs in the dark, where no one could see, your fingers touching me, massaging me, making me wet." He groans through the phone, and I feel a stab of satisfaction tempered by the fact I'm so turned on it hurts.

"I'd think about you fingering me during the movie, and then later, at home, I'd make myself come thinking about your mouth touching me all the places your fingers did."

"Jesus fuck, O." Jamie sounds utterly wrecked. I have no time to contemplate if I've gone too far, too soon, because he says—nearly growls, actually— "I want that. I want to touch every inch of you. Then I want to go over each inch again with my mouth, my tongue. I want to make you feel so good. I'm going to take my sweet time. I want you wet and aching and desperate for me, Ophelia. Only me."

The bald statement shocks me, not because it's offensive. I'm throbbing between my legs in anticipation of him touching me.

We haven't even kissed yet, and he's already the best sex I've ever had.

"That sounds—good." Understatement of the century.

"When can I see you?"

Part of me wants to demand that he drop everything and come over and make good on his promise right this instant. The rest of me isn't ready to move quite that fast with the man who until two days ago was merely my annoyingly attractive best guy friend.

"I'll see you at the party. Sunday." That's two days away. Two days for me to get my head on straight and my libido under control.

"All right. Sunday. And Ophelia, I meant what I said before."

"Which part?"

"All of it. But the part about not doing anything you don't want to do. I know this is unusual for you."

"Ha." He's not wrong, but maybe he thinks I'm more of an innocent than I am. "You know I'm not a virgin, right?"

"Okay. I'm not a virgin either."

I snort at his matter-of-fact tone.

"I'll see you Sunday."

"See you then, O."

I lie there for a long time, stuck between the hormones and adrenaline of our near-phone-sex and confessions, and terror at what I've done. There's no going back now. And on Sunday, I'm the one who's going to have to make the next move.

CHAPTER 18

JAMIE

It's almost a carbon copy of the Super Bowl party. Here we are again, on a Sunday afternoon at Nicole and Ricky's, except instead of a football game we're being subjected to an award show and instead of chips and a Tex-Mex buffet, we're being plied with mini quiches and bacon-wrapped dates. Not that I'm complaining.

"We're auditioning the caterers for the wedding," Ricky explains when I ask why they're having another party.

"Ah. Can't you guys do a tasting like a normal couple?"

The look he gives me says, "What do you think?" But he doesn't really mind. And his willingness to indulge his soon-to-be wife says good things about their future marriage, I think. Nicole knows what she wants, she knows how to get it, and Ricky's purpose in life seems to be making her happy, so it's a win-win.

"You look sharp, by the way," Ricky says, looking me over.

Despite my grumping to Ophelia, I do have something besides jeans and hoodies in my closet, so here I am in a pair of slacks and a light green button-down shirt. No tie, obviously. It's too warm for a jacket, and I bailed on breakfast club yesterday in favor of getting a haircut so my hair isn't flopping into my eyes as much as it usually does. Missing the weekly gathering of design geeks might have had something to do with not wanting to share a meal with Ophelia's dad twelve hours after hearing her detailed sex fantasies about me. Blame it on self-preservation.

"I worked out some of the bugs on the printer commands today. Should be ready for trials soon." With effort, I tell Ricky about the progress I've made on my printer instead of asking about Ophelia's whereabouts. She usually cares more about dissecting what the stars are wearing than the actual awards, so I kind of assumed she'd be here for the red carpet, but she's nowhere to be seen.

I wonder for the millionth time if she's going to try to wriggle out of this, pretend nothing happened and act like we're still Jamie and Ophelia, friends forever.

After the things we said, I think that ship has sailed.

But God, I need to find out what's going to happen next.

A stream of guests arrive, mostly work contacts of Ricky's, and I pace around, barely paying attention to the buzz of conversation and the award show no one is watching.

Could she have gotten a flat tire? Run out of gas? Did she stumble and dislocate another toe? As I'm reaching for my phone, she sweeps in the front door, looking pristinely put together and almost more beautiful than I can stand.

I consume her in one greedy glance, then take longer to appreciate her pink cheeks, her dewy lips, her body wrapped in a silvery pink dress made of something silky and weightless. She'd said something recently about finding an old ballet costume in a thrift shop. This must be it. Its bodice clings to her curves. The skirt is huge and impractical, but short, showing off her legs. She wears ballet flats with ribbons tied up the calf. The sweet bondage look definitely becomes her.

Before I can form any sort of greeting, Nicole and some of the other female guests squeal over her.

"You look like a princess!" Nicole exclaims.

Ophelia isn't a princess. She's a queen. I'm underdressed and overwhelmed, a mere peon.

She laughs off the girls' attention and meets my gaze. Her cheeks seem to grow pinker. Is it because I can't hide the admiration in my eyes? Or because she likes what she sees?

Either way, I can't help crossing to her, taking her gently by the elbow and giving her a slightly too long kiss on the cheek. She smells like sugarcoated rose petals. I want to eat her up.

I hesitate before speaking because everything that comes to my mind is entirely inappropriate for the mixed company. *I want you. We belong together. I love*—no, don't even go there. I settle for an entirely inadequate, "Hey."

"Hey," she says back. There's a beat where we look into each other's eyes and something deep and unspoken zips between us. I'm saying, *Why are we stopping ourselves? Let's get out of here and do this.* And she's saying. *Please, not yet.*

I can live with the promise of that silent *yet.*

I back off, nod toward the bar. "Are you drinking?"

"I better not," she says. "Never know when you're going to have to take a narcotic."

I snort out a laugh, remembering the last disastrous theme party.

"Then let's get you something soft." We walk to the bar together, beauty and the geek.

"You look lovely," Ricky greets Ophelia a bit too loudly, in that slightly cringey way he gets with his bro friends. Several of them are crowding around his latest boutique whiskey acquisition. I love Ricky to death, but sometimes he really lives up to the capitalist stereotype, with his whiskey drinking, golf playing, and legal gambling in the form of investing. If Nicole wouldn't kill him, he'd probably smoke cigars, too. I'm more the beer and occasional joint type.

One of Ricky's guests, who I've been introduced to a couple times and whose name I still can't remember, tears himself away from his single-malt long enough to eye Ophelia up and down in the way that used to be considered wolfish and is now laughably passé. "She sure does," he agrees.

"Actually, I was talking about Jamie," Ricky says easily.

That's why I love him—he comes through in unexpected moments. I laugh and shift a shade closer to O.

The bro smirks at me, apparently not put off by Ricky's irreverence. "I didn't know sneakers and slacks from Kohl's did it for you, Ricky."

I don't have time to be offended because Ophelia speaks up. "Works for me."

I flash her a smile.

"Whatever," Broseph says, staring at Ophelia's chest. "You work for me, baby."

"All right, I'm cutting you off, Jeff," Ricky says. "That's my future cousin-in-law." He starts to steer Jeff away from the bar toward the food.

"You said there would be girls at this party," Jeff says to Ricky grumpily. "She's the only one I see."

"Your flattery needs work, Jeff," Ophelia says dryly. "As does your pickup game."

"Maybe if you weren't a frigid child, you wouldn't get offended at a simple compliment," Jeff sneers.

Ricky and I both freeze and I glance at my cousin. We're not above a little physical intimidation when it comes to defending the women in our lives, but it turns out that it's not necessary.

"You'll never have the privilege of finding out if I'm frigid or not, and between the two of us, you're the child." Her delivery is calm and collected, and that's the thing about Ophelia. She looks like a dandelion, soft and gentle and like a light breeze would blow her over, but she's fucking tough as nails.

Jeff's doing a passable imitation of a fish caught on a line, opening and closing his mouth ineffectually. She's stunned him into silence.

"I'm calling you a ride," Ricky says as he helps poor Jeff toward the front door.

"Well done," I say to Ophelia. "What an asshole."

"Thanks." Then she literally shakes her shoulders and straightens up, as if she's brushed him off and is ready to move on. She's magnificent.

"I think I'll take something slightly stronger than water," she says.

The other whiskey-drinking bros have scattered in the wake of Jeff's humiliation, so I swing under the partition and play bartender.

"What's your poison?" I pretend to scan the bottles on offer, but I'm really waiting for her to say something—anything—to give me a clue about what she's thinking. I find myself leaning toward her; she smells so good, I'm practically getting a contact high.

Instead of answering she puts her chin in the cradle of her hands and sighs. I figure she's working up to something, so I grab a Stella and pop the top. I don't feel much like drinking it, but I don't want her to drink alone.

"I'm frigid," she says quietly, "just because I don't want to have sex with every guy who hits on me. But if I slept with every guy who hit on me, he wouldn't call me frigid. He'd call me a slut. It's so disheartening that no matter what a woman does, she gets labeled. It's like the only acceptable option is to be in a sexual, monogamous relationship that will someday end in marriage." She frowns. "Can you blame me for opting out?"

I don't respond right away. Maybe this is one of those girl

conversations where they want to talk and be heard and not actually engage in a dialogue.

"I wish people would quit judging other people's life choices. What's it to you if I don't want to get married? You'll never have to buy me a blender and be forced to listen to an '80s cover band for four hours."

I'm pretty sure the "you" she's referring to is universal, not specifically me, but I still picture being invited to Ophelia's wedding—to someone else. The idea makes my stomach churn. I don't know if I could do it. But that's not what she means.

"I like '80s cover bands," I say instead. "And aren't you obsessed with the B-52s?"

"That's not the point. Of course *you'd* like that," she says with a pout. "But a lot of other people don't get the genius that is 'Love Shack.' We'd totally dig an '80s cover band at our wedding."

I smile slowly at her and her eyes widen as she realizes what she said. She makes a face. "You know what I mean."

"Right."

"Not that we're—obviously that's not—I didn't mean..." She's flustered, and I take pity.

"You don't ever have to get married, O. And I'll never judge you for your life choices. I promise." I adjust my glasses unnecessarily for something to do with my hands. "But there's a difference between not believing in marriage and keeping yourself sequestered from the rest of the world. And I say that in the most nonjudgmental way possible."

She's quiet.

"For the record, I know you are not frigid. And it's already been established that you aren't a slut." She smiles a little, and I know she's remembering our conversation a few days earlier. "You defy their shitty labels. You're the warmest, most alive person I know. Look at you: You are a hibiscus in winter." To me, she's the brightest thing in the room. She glows. "I'm lucky to get to be around you. I always have been. Whether or not we end up in a sexual, monogamous relationship won't change that. I promise."

I pass her my untouched Stella. "I'm going to see who won best sound mixing."

And I leave her staring vacantly at the bottle of beer.

CHAPTER 19
OPHELIA

I knew I'd regret coming. After the Super Bowl debacle, I had no business attending another of Nicole and Ricky's theme parties. Jeff's casual insult hurt less than a dislocated toe, but it still hurt. Yes, it was banal and chauvinistic. But a girl who's put on a special dress and fancy shoes and done her makeup and wants her best guy friend to think she's pretty doesn't want to be accused of being a frigid child.

I don't feel frigid. After Jamie's sweet words across the bar, I'm positively melting.

We're supposed to be watching the award show, but I couldn't care less. I slide off my bar stool, bypass the living room entirely, and find Nicole in the kitchen where she's coordinating with the caterer.

"Can I talk to you for a sec?"

"Is it the bacon-wrapped dates? Too rich, right? That's what I told Marta. Don't worry, the mini chocolate cheesecakes are really yummy."

"It's not about the food."

She stops fussing with a tray of appetizers and looks at me more closely.

"I'm sorry about Jeff. Ricky told me what happened."

I flush, wondering how Ricky described the interaction to Nicole. "What did he say?"

"Only that Jeff was an ass and you took care of it."

I flush again, this time with pride. I am proud of how I managed the situation, but I still don't want to spend more time thinking about it than I have to. "Ricky shouldn't serve whiskey if his friends can't hold their liquor."

"Good point. And don't worry, he's not invited to the wedding. I think Ricky might not renew his contract anyway."

"Whatever. I don't care about Jeff. I need to know what to do about Jamie."

"Oh! Right! Wait." She indicates to the beleaguered caterer that she wants the rest of the sweet potato pancakes to go out, then pulls me around the corner into her walk-in pantry for some privacy. "How's it going?"

I had filled Nicole in on some of the details of my phone call with Jamie. Not the sex stuff, but the fact that we were moving inexorably toward something unprecedented. She was supportive, but candid. "I love Jamie," she'd said, "but if he hurts you, I'm not going to be happy." From someone else, that would have been a mild statement, but from Nicole, it's tantamount to a death threat. No one wants to see Nicole when she's not happy.

"It's weird. One minute, we're acting normally, having fun; the next moment he says something that shakes me to my core. And the crazy thing is, we haven't even kissed yet. He told me I have to make the first move."

"He *told* you?" Nicole raises her eyebrows.

"Not, like, in a bossy way. He's giving me all the power. But I don't know if I can handle it. That's why I don't do this stuff." I allow myself a whiny moment since it's Nic I'm complaining to. "It's been so long since I kissed anyone. What if I suck at it?"

Nicole grabs me by the shoulders and literally shakes me. "Listen. You can do this. You are Ophelia Jane Winesap. You have the name of a Victorian heroine, but you are a 21ˢᵗ-century woman. You take down assholes with pithy comebacks. You pioneer technological innovations to better our schools and enrich children's lives. You're the best maid of honor in the history of weddings. You march out there, you kiss Jamie Kendell on the mouth, and you don't come back until you have no lipstick left."

I laugh loudly, and impulsively throw my arms around my cousin and squeeze. I'm not known for my public displays of affection, but Nicole just hugs me back tightly.

"Thanks for the pep talk," I whisper.

"Anytime, honey."

As we emerge from the pantry I swipe two mini chocolate cheesecakes from a platter, then locate Jamie on the couch, talking to Kate, one of Nicole's other bridesmaids. She lives in L.A. and I haven't seen her since Nicole and Ricky's engagement party. I allow myself a stab of envy at her looks—lush, long red hair, tall and built and looking like a grownup in tight jeans, ankle boots, and a simple but probably expensive white T-shirt. For a moment I feel like a little girl playing dress-up in my thrift store ballet costume, then I remember that Kate's one of the nicest, coolest people I've ever met. I let go of my irrational jealousy that she's talking with my...Jamie.

"Hey, Ophelia, or should I say, greetings, Swan Queen? You look stunning. How are you, girl?" Kate's up and hugging me, and it's all I can do to avoid smearing her white shirt with the chocolate cheesecakes in my hands.

"I'm fine. I didn't know you would be here."

"Passing through town. Nicole's putting me up tonight."

"I thought I'd have to wait until the bachelorette extravaganza to see you."

Kate sighs dramatically. "Ah, yes, the bachelorette weekend. No simple party for our Nic. We have to spend seventy-two straight hours with her to prove our undying womanly devotion to the impending bride."

"Girls are weird," Jamie says. "I'm pretty sure Ricky's bachelor party is going to be an evening of whiskey and cigars."

"Actually, I heard he's planning a weekend backpacking trip to the Sierra Nevadas—or was it Yosemite?" Kate says, a twinkle in her eye.

"What, seriously?" Jamie is not amused. He's relatively outdoorsy, but I giggle imagining him trying to wrangle a bunch of Ricky's finance friends up a trail.

"Relax, James," I say, putting him out of his misery. "The weekend commitment is for the girls only."

He makes a face when he realizes we've been putting him on.

"O, are you holding something that appears to be made of sugar and fat?" Jamie nods toward the cheesecakes.

Oh, yeah. Despite my best efforts at procrastinating, I actually had planned to whisk Jamie away someplace we could be alone. I suppose I can't put it off any longer, and my gut buzzes with nerves. "I stole some dessert."

"Dessert! Nicole's been holding out on me," Kate grumbles.

"She's got tons in the kitchen. Go bug her to let the caterer bring them out," I suggest, half-hoping she'll stay put so I won't have to go through with the marvelous, terrible plan of kissing my best friend.

"Don't tell me twice," she says. In an instant, she's gone and so is my human shield.

My mouth goes dry when I glance back at Jamie. He looks exceptionally handsome tonight. He's had a haircut since I saw him last, which makes him look less like an overgrown teenager and more like a man. Man-Jamie makes me flustered and hot and want things. His tongue darts out a little way and touches lightly against his full bottom lip. I drag my gaze from his mouth to his eyes and I can tell he knows what I'm thinking. He nods slightly. Okay. We're doing this.

After all, the worst thing that could happen is we destroy our friendship and cause a lot of collateral damage.

I tip my head toward the glass doors to the patio. "Want to..."

"Yes."

I feel that yes all the way down to my toes. That yes is permission for me to do whatever I want. To have whatever I want. To take whatever I want. I wish I'd actually consumed a glass of something alcoholic to explain the floaty feeling suffusing my body, but I have nothing to blame except Jamie and my palpable attraction toward him.

I step outside and goose bumps appear on my bare arms. Nicole and Ricky's backyard was recently torn apart and redesigned by Rosie's plant-genius boyfriend Gus as an early wedding present. It's been transformed from a water-sucking English garden into a drought-friendly modern landscape more suitable for Santa Barbara's dry Mediterranean climate.

I walk over to the requisite midcentury modern patio set and contemplate seating arrangements. If I sit on one of the armchairs, Jamie will take the other, and we could end up dancing around each other all night. So I choose the bench, leaving plenty of room for Jamie to sit beside me. I look up at him and hold up a hand.

"Cheesecake?"

He frowns. He probably thinks I'm teasing him. I am, in a way. But he's given me the power to set the pace, and I'm going to use it.

When he doesn't answer, I take a bite. Velvety chocolate explodes on my tongue. The moan I let out is only half-exaggerated.

"Good?" His voice is strangled.

I hum my response and finish off the cake. Then I pat the space beside me. He obeys, sitting no closer than when we eat our lunch together, but in the dark it feels ten times more intimate. I offer him the second cheesecake. He takes it as he did on Valentine's Day, in one gigantic bite. I want to touch him, but I let my hands fall to my sides.

I watch in the dark as he swallows. I can't stop looking at his lips. His mouth would taste like chocolate.

"So, what do you think?" I ask.

He's as distracted as me, because he cocks his head. "About what?"

"The cheesecake." Desserts have always been safe territory for us.

"Sweet. Dense."

"Um, you are talking about the dessert, right?" It's sort of a joke, but I may sound a tiny bit defensive.

"Sure." He smiles, then. "What do *you* think?"

"I don't know," I whisper.

"What are we doing out here, Ophelia? Because I can't play around with..." He pauses, gesturing between us.

"I know." God. I'm ruining it before I can even start. "Give me a minute."

He doesn't say anything—he's giving me my minute. He gives me so much and I don't know if I can accept the responsibility he's entrusting me with. I should be the one worried about getting hurt, but I know that in this relationship I could very well be the one who's going to end up stomping all over his heart.

"Maybe this isn't a good—" Even in the dark I can see the flash of hurt on his face. If I don't act now, I might not get another chance. I square my shoulders. "Okay, wait. Just wait." I glance at my shoes. It's the safest place to look. "I think I need to be much drunker to do this."

"You haven't drunk anything tonight."

"I know."

"That's good."

"Why?"

"I don't want you to be able to blame this on alcohol."

"Blame what on alcohol?"

"Kissing me."

"We haven't kissed," I say. The "yet" hovers on the tip of my tongue but I don't want to give him the satisfaction.

"We will."

I drag my gaze off my feet and back to his face. My eyes have adjusted to the darkness and I can see him better now, his slightly crooked nose, his pupils taking over almost his entire iris, his Adam's apple peeking out of the collar of his shirt.

"If we're doing this promise me you'll tell me if you aren't happy. You can walk away. Don't be afraid of that. From this point on, tell me and we'll call it a day. We'll stay friends. It'll be fine."

"Okay." He sounds like he's agreeing with a crazy person.

I play my last card. "You know, we could kiss and it could be...gross."

"Gross?" He sounds skeptical, and I have to agree I'm grasping at straws.

"It might be like kissing your sister."

"I don't have a sister."

"I know. Me either. I mean, we're both only children. Obviously. I meant—"

"There's only one way to find out."

He has a point.

I'm out of excuses.

I think about Miss Rumphius. Sure, she didn't need a man. But she was brave. She went after what she wanted. I want Jamie. I can be brave, too.

I face him, my silly ballet skirt floating up around my knees.

It's been so long since I've kissed anyone. I move mostly on instinct, blood thrumming in my ears. The air between us thickens, until suddenly there's no more air, and my lips are pressed against his. This is it. I'm kissing Jamie.

What do I do now?

CHAPTER 20

JAMIE

I'm a little shocked she actually kissed me. Ophelia surprises me yet again.

Her kiss is so sweet and soft that I don't want to move and ruin the perfection of the moment. But then it all hits me. Ophelia is kissing me, like, right this very nanosecond. The thing I've dreamed of for months, for *years*, is finally happening.

I have to have more.

Just like that the kiss goes from sweet, chaste, to something hotter, deeper. I open my mouth, suck her bottom lip in, and the rest follows from there. Tongues. Lips. Hot breath. Pent-up yearning all exploding into one searing, needy kiss.

It's too much, too fast, for both of us, and we break apart.

I swear nearly inaudibly, incapable of deeper verbal communication. The color has risen in O's cheeks, and her chest rises and falls as fast as a hummingbird's. This time, it's me who moves toward her, settling my lips over hers. Slowly I learn the curve of her lips. I uncover her essence under the faint taste of chocolate on her tongue.

My hands skim up the line of her throat. One makes a home at the base of her skull, cupping her hair, feeling her ubiquitous bun slip out of its knots, maybe helping it along a little. With my other hand I can't stop exploring her petal-soft skin, the shell of her ear, the parabola of her shoulder, bare except for the silky strap holding up her flouncy costume.

My blood has heated up past the boiling point and every cell in my body is crying to take this further. I'm aching to lay Ophelia down, strip her naked, and make her mine in every way. The analytical part of my brain beats my primitive urges into submission with effort. We're not animals, and Ophelia isn't mine to have. Not yet.

I break off the kiss and look down at her. Her eyes are still closed, her mouth parted in a pout made for kissing.

I want to tell her so many things. That I think about her all the time. That she's precious to me. That as far as I'm concerned we're made for each other and we should put our nonsense behind us and start building a life together. That she kisses like an angel. That I've never wanted anyone as much as I want her.

Problem is, saying any one of those things would be enough to send her running for the hills.

I swallow my words and try for casual. "What's the verdict?"

"Hmmm?"

I'm gratified to see her eyes are glassy, unfocused.

"You know, was it gross, or…?"

"Not gross, no. Can't pretend kissing you is like kissing my brother. Unfortunately." She sounds too composed, so I grab her hands and hold them in mine before she starts to slip away from me.

"Not gross for me, either."

"Okay, so what do we do, now that we know we're not grossed out by each other?"

This conversation is a bit ridiculous, but keeping things light means there's less chance of us making some irrevocably bad move.

"Let's keep doing what we usually do," I say, stroking her knuckles with my thumbs lightly. "Except if one of us feels like kissing the other, we'll ask the other person if that's okay, and then...kiss."

"That sounds sensible."

"Sensible," I repeat dutifully. It does sound rather sickeningly sensible. When I kiss her I use all my senses, but I'm far from sensible.

"Okay, let's try it." She closes her eyes. "Kiss me, please."

I don't have to be told twice.

Many minutes later, it hits me that we've spent the evening making out in my cousin's backyard. I'd say it makes me feel like a teenager, except I had no hope of landing a girl like Ophelia in the dark days of pubescent acne and campaigning to be president of the engineering club. Luckily, college was broadening in more than one respect, and I know what I'm doing in the kissing department. Ophelia, her mouth pink and kiss-swollen, seems to have no complaints.

"I guess we should go in?" she says eventually.

"If you want." I gesture to her hair, delightfully mussed. "But everyone is going to know that something not gross happened between us after they take one look at you."

"Ugh. I forgot about the gossip mill."

Not only are Ophelia and I playing with our own lives and happiness, but what we do affects the people we love, too. Given half a chance, Ricky and Nicole will be planning our wedding as soon as they finish with their own extravaganza. What if we get together then break up? What would it do to our family?

"I should get home," Ophelia says. "Work tomorrow."

"Me too."

There's a silence. I know her so well, but I have no idea what she's thinking right now.

"Lunch tomorrow?"

"Absolutely," I say, relieved our normal routine is intact.

She stands up, and I can't not touch her now that she's given her consent. I rise and wrap my arms around her. We've hugged before, but I let myself linger, let myself really feel the press of her body against mine. Nothing's changed—I'm still there for her in all the ways I was before. But now there's more.

She's stiff in my arms at first, then relaxes against me. I drop a kiss to the top of her head, she rubs her cheek against my chest like a cat. Then she steps away and it's over.

She goes inside without looking back at me. I have no idea what she'll say or if we're telling people or what we'd tell them. I'm not in the habit of broadcasting my personal life all over the place, and Ophelia is even more close-lipped than me. But Nicole will know instantly, if she doesn't already.

I slip out to the street through the side yard without saying any goodbyes. I need to get home in order to take care of the raging hard-on I've had since the moment Ophelia's lips touched mine. I'll be thinking of her, and this time, I won't feel guilty for coming with her name on my lips.

CHAPTER 21

OPHELIA

Standing under the scalding spray of the shower Monday morning, I scour my skin raw as if to atone for my stupidity. Being in a sexual relationship with someone I care about is too far outside my comfort zone. I'm bound to screw something up and hurt Jamie. That, or I'm at risk of having my heart broken into a million little pieces that can never be put back together again.

Either way, no pressure, right?

I turn off the water and throw together an outfit of leggings, boots, a tea-length dress, and my trusty duster. I'm wrapping a scarf around my neck when I hear a bang and rattle on the other side of my bedroom door. I'm momentarily frightened, but then I think, *Jamie?*

His name is on the tip of my tongue when I open the door to confront my intruder. I swallow it back when I see Nicole and Kate bumbling around my kitchen.

"What the fuck are you two doing here?"

"Where the fuck is your coffee maker?" Nicole is way too salty for someone who's breaking and entering, but since she rarely swears she must really need caffeine.

"It's fucking broken." I nudge her aside and plug in my electric kettle. I've been surviving on English Breakfast and the coffee maker in the teachers lounge.

"Are you fucking kidding me?" she complains as I pull out three mugs.

"If you're going to break into my house you might as well fucking bring coffee!"

"Calm the fuck down, you two," Kate yells. Then we all start laughing hysterically.

Soon tea is steaming in our mugs, and Nicole's contribution of last night's leftover desserts are making their way into our stomachs in lieu of breakfast. I repeat my earlier question. "Seriously, though, what the fuck are you doing here?"

Kate smirks, and Nicole sticks out her tongue. We're so classy.

"I think you know, O. You ran out last night with barely a word, after spending hours alone with a man on the patio."

"What is this, Regency England? Am I going to be ruined now?" I grimace. I do feel a bit like my reputation has taken a hit. I'm notorious for not dating. People draw their own conclusions—that I'm picky, that I'm shy, that I'm asexual. What business is it of theirs?

"We want the scoop," Kate says, licking éclair filling off her fingers. "And I want to know if he's as good a kisser as I imagined."

"You imagined kissing Jamie?" This comes out a little sharper than I mean it to.

Kate laughs, ever chill. "Don't worry, O. It was a passing, one-sided wondering, nothing more. So give it up."

"We need details," Nicole adds.

"Hurry, because I have to drive back to L.A. before lunch. And don't you have to go to work?"

I check my phone for the time. "In twelve minutes."

"Spill!"

If you can't tell your friends about the cute boy you kissed last night, who can you tell? I look down into my mug. Speaking to an inanimate object feels less overwhelming.

"The kiss was—weird. Objectively, it was a good kiss—yes, he's a good kisser, Kate—but because it was with Jamie, specifically, it made it better. Like finding a winning lottery ticket at the bottom of your purse. Something wonderful and magical had been there all the time and you almost missed it because it was too familiar. I thought I knew him so well, but I must've been beyond obtuse, because that kind of connection doesn't happen overnight. This must have been simmering for a long time, but now it feels like it's happening so fast. All we've done is kiss, and I'm certain I'm going to screw it up, but I can't take it back and I don't want to. Yeah, the kissing—epically good. He's very focused. Thorough. And his hands!" I shiver and finally look up from my tea.

The girls stare at me and sigh in unison like lovestruck cartoon characters.

"You asked," I say, my defenses up.

"No, that was marvelous," Nicole says softly. "You aren't going to screw it up. He's crazy about you. I'd say you have a lot of leeway."

"Focused and thorough. Not surprised. And girl, you are lucky," Kate adds.

I nod. She'd know, having lost her fiancé in an accident shortly before their wedding. Having Jamie in my life was amazing enough when we were only friends, and now I get to have that, plus kissing. Probably more.

I'd like to get Nicole's and Kate's perspective on the "more" part. It's been so long since I had sex with another human being that I've sort of forgotten how one gets from here to there. Not that it's rocket science. But we're out of time, and I hustle the girls out the door before I'm late for work.

"Another one bites the dust," Kate whispers to me when

Nicole's halfway to her car. I jerk my gaze up to her and she winks at me. Damn bridesmaids.

I want to protest. I'm not getting into a relationship like the one we Never a Brides swore we'd never have. This is different. This isn't marriage. Jamie knows I'm not interested in getting married.

I'm about to say something to that effect, but Kate gives me another cheeky wink and a hug and says, "I'm happy for you."

That scares me. Because I'm happy, too. And that can only mean that unhappiness lies right around the corner.

CHAPTER 22

JAMIE

It's Saturday morning, almost a week after I first touched Ophelia with carnal intent on the patio at Ricky and Nicole's Oscar party. I wish I could say the morning begins with me waking up next to my girlfriend, Ophelia, after making love to her into the small hours, rousing her for a bout of morning sex, followed by a leisurely breakfast and maybe a walk on the beach.

Unfortunately, I wake up the way I always do—alone in my own bed, morning wood more persistent than usual.

I don't think I can call Ophelia my girlfriend. The truth is, I've barely seen her all week. We had lunch on Monday—totally normal except for a clumsy attempt at a hello kiss by me, and a lot of blushing and stammering on her end. I know she hasn't done this in a while, but she's so exceptionally effective in the other areas of her life, I figured she'd be as ruthlessly efficient in this one, too. But she seems shy.

It's actually kind of cute. I think everything she does is kind of cute, even when it's annoying. And I'm not a dick who needs to rush to get in her pants now that there's a green light. I can wait as long as it takes. It's just that I've wanted this for so long, I thought maybe we could move a *smidgeon* faster.

Our lunch dates are not helping. We see each other, talk, eat. And then we kiss for about ten seconds, but we're in public so we can't get too hot and heavy, and I don't want to walk back into work at a museum filled with children with a hard-on. Just, no.

We need privacy, even if we take things molasses slow. I can happily imagine taking my time to explore every peach-soft inch of her. But when I tried to make a date with her for Friday night she put me off—some work party that sounded half made-up. She finally agreed to go out with me tonight, hours from now, which means I'm free to attend my usual Saturday morning get-together.

I have a standing date at Jack's Diner, a dive that, God willing, will never become trendy with millennial tourists. On any given Saturday morning a bunch of older gentlemen trundle into Jack's, order the two-egg breakfast combo, and the coffee and conversation flow. I'm the youngest attendee by about thirty years, the next oldest being Andy, Ophelia's dad, who was my sponsor, bringing me here for the first time a little over a year ago.

He's at the usual table talking with Sterling, a retired Santa Barbara High auto shop teacher, and Mike, who's also retired after running his own custom surfboard shop for about a million years. His daughter runs it now, and he keeps his hand in, but mostly he putters around.

That's what these guys do: putter. Andy's a champion putterer, which is why he fits in with the older guys though he's only in his mid-fifties. And me? I've been known to putter, but I'm saving my major puttering for my prime puttering years—a few decades away, at least.

These old guys are the original makers: woodworkers, welders, painters. They made careers making stuff that people use, then taught the next generations. Some of the tools have changed—we use 3D printers and design apps more than planes and saws, but you have to know how those work, too.

When we've had our fill of coffee and old-man gossip, Andy and I go for our usual stroll from Jack's down the beach to the other end of the harbor and back. Sometimes we talk about Ophelia. He always seems starved for information about her. It's not like they're estranged, but I see him nearly every week and she easily goes a month without a face-to-face visit.

We walk under a cloudless blue sky. My mind is on Ophelia. This week hasn't gone at all like I hoped it would, and yet simply having been able to touch her has been incredible. I'm so lost in my own thoughts that hearing her name from someone else's lips startles me, and I almost lose my footing.

"Ophelia and I are having brunch tomorrow," Andy mentions casually. He's got a fisherman's cap pulled over his graying head and I can't see his eyes.

"Oh? That's good." She's probably going to tell him about us, not that there's much to tell.

I wonder how Andy would react to knowing the depth of my feelings for his daughter. I've always been careful to make it seem like we are what we are: good friends, nothing more, nothing less. But Andy's not obtuse. Still, something like this should come from his daughter, not from me.

"Was thinking of taking her to the Biltmore, do it up fancy."

"Why? She'd be happy at Jack's," I say.

"It's the first time she's asked me to meet up with her in more than a year. Usually I have to be the one to ask her."

I hadn't realized things were so distant between them, and I don't know what to say.

"She's never quite forgiven me, or her mother." There's no regret in his voice. It's matter-of-fact. He's an artist, but he doesn't wear his emotions on his sleeve.

"Oh."

"We were all so close once upon a time. It was too good to

last, I suppose. Or maybe we weren't as happy as we thought. I knew things weren't right between her mother and me, but I could ignore it when we had O to focus on. But she grew up, and the reasons for Helen and me to stay together got thinner and thinner. O never forgave us for not being—"

He stops, both talking and walking, and turns to stare out over the slate gray ocean. I need him to continue, to tell me. Maybe it will help me figure out what's holding Ophelia and me back.

"For not being—?"

"For not being soul mates."

"Soul mates?" That's not what I thought he was going to say.

He laughs. "Sorry, I guess I have love on the brain."

"Yeah?" I laugh uncomfortably. So do I.

"Tell me about your progress with the prototype." We talk shop all the way back.

Later, the phrase he used echoes over and over again in my head. *Soul mates.* Is that what Ophelia and I are? Do I believe in that? Does she? Maybe she did once upon a time.

The disaster of this week is not going to stop me. I've been tentative, letting her lead, and she's been doing a piss-poor job of it. Now it's my turn.

CHAPTER 23

OPHELIA

I've changed my clothes three times since I got home from my usual Saturday routine of grocery shopping, laundry, and gassing up my car. Jamie said he'd pick me up at six. Our first official date.

I have no right to be nervous. We've been out a million times before, just us—dinners, parties, drinks, movies, concerts. We've been on dozens of proto-dates. This isn't different.

Except it is.

I won't have to wonder if his searching glances have a deeper meaning. I won't have to scold myself for noticing how good he smells or avoid double entendres. He'll know that I selected this precise shade of lipstick with the knowledge that our lips will be touching at some point in the evening. As I slide the tube of Passion Pop into my purse, I feel lightheaded. I'm nearly hyperventilating. Not an auspicious beginning.

I'm aware that the week hasn't gone especially well. We've somehow lost the ease we used to have around each other. I have to believe we can get it back. Nicole gave me a pep talk when I called her in a panic right around outfit change number two.

"Less thinking, more doing. Less talking, more kissing. Men are simple. Don't overcomplicate it."

Not bad advice, really. Jamie has a brilliant brain, but he's still a guy. So I pick my short emerald green dress with the flared skirt and heeled sandals. Now I have plenty of leg showing to distract him from my inadequacies in other areas.

At six on the dot he's knocking on my door and I grab my purse and coat, but when I open up, I can see my effort to look nice for the clichéd dinner date I had envisioned has gone to waste. Jamie holds a canvas bag of groceries in one arm and a spray of flowers in the other.

I blink away unexpected tears and take the flowers. They're lupines.

"My favorite."

"I know," he says. He leans in and kisses me on the cheek, lingering for the barest moment before he's all business again. "Change of plans. We're having a night in." Then he shoulders past me and into the kitchen. "I'll cook, you mix the drinks and pick the music."

"Deal." I generally enjoy cooking, but I'm not going to turn down someone else making me dinner.

I ask my smart speaker to play M83 and dump some dried-up Trader Joe's daffodils out of my only vase to make a home for my new bouquet.

"Where did you get these? I never see them." Lupines are not native to Southern California. I've never seen them in the wild. Another one of those things I'm going to get around to doing when I'm older, braver, stronger, wiser, etc.

"I know a guy," Jamie says as he starts chopping. The pungent scent of cilantro fills the small space. I glance over and see cabbage, tilapia, and tortillas. Suddenly I'm starving and happy.

I freeze in the act of opening up the cupboard where I keep

my small stash of liquor. Happy. I tip my head to the side, considering.

Let's go with happy for a little while, shall we?

"You have a lupine guy? And what goes with fish tacos? Should we break out the cerveza?"

"Maybe margaritas?"

"Or caipirnhas," I say, feeling like something different. "Ingrid got me hooked on them after her vacation to Rio. I think I still have some cachaça."

A little while later we're sitting on my couch, holding plates of steaming fish wrapped in corn tortillas, along with shredded cabbage and special sauce, ice cold caipis on the coffee table. He tells me about the latest gossip from the museum, and I rave about the tacos. "Better than that food truck that one time where the tacos were so good but we couldn't remember the name and still haven't been able to track down."

"High praise."

"So, why'd you want to stay in?" I ask, though I'm pretty sure I know why.

"This week has been pretty crazy busy. We've been rushed." He sets his plate down. "And I promised you that I'd take my time."

I swallow, feeling hot even though the room isn't warm. "You did."

"I like your dress," he says.

"Thanks."

"I love your clothes. Maybe that sounds weird coming from me, but I like it that you don't look like everyone else in their jeans and hoodies."

"Even though that's all you wear?" To be fair, tonight he's wearing jeans and a long-sleeved gray T-shirt in some insanely soft-looking fabric. I want to touch it. I'm allowed now. Tentatively, I run my hand over his forearm.

"Your shirt is soft," I say, kind of idiotically. It is, but it's his arm that I'm really feeling, hard and firm underneath. I don't know how he can be so adorably geeky but still fill out his shirts so nicely. "How do you get these muscles? Are you secretly a gym rat?"

He shrugs, letting me run my fingers over him, letting me explore. "Good genes, I guess."

"Right. Then why are you blind as a bat without your glasses?"

"I made a deal when they were whipping up my DNA combo—I traded eyesight for effortless muscles."

"Huh. Most guys would have asked for something else." My gaze drops to his lap.

"Oh, I had to give up straight teeth for that," he jokes.

"What are you talking about? You have toothpaste-commercial teeth."

"After three years of braces."

"They were that crooked?"

"Yeah, but it was worth it," he says, voice low and teasing. And I realize he's alluding to the size of his...

"This is a ridiculous conversation." I take my hand off his arm and take a sip of my drink, which has been watered down by melting ice.

"Pretty much." He laughs. "But I like teasing you."

"I...I don't know how to do this," I confess. "I feel like I've been playacting all night."

"Acting?" His teasing look has been replaced by concern.

"The part of the flirty girl trying to get a boy to like her."

"I already like you," he says immediately. "I thought we were having fun."

"We were. We are. It's just not...relaxing."

"Things are changing. It's normal for there to be an adjustment period."

"I guess I miss things being easy between us."

"O, things might have seemed easy, but didn't you feel, I don't know, on edge with me before? I sure as hell did."

"Sometimes," I admit. "But then I thought my brain was wanting to see things that weren't there. This is feeling tingly and nervous and—"

"I make you nervous?"

"Sort of."

"Hmm. That could be a good thing." He sets his drink down and takes my hands in his. "This thing between us, it's new, and it's different, and it's not always going to feel comfortable. I don't want it to feel comfortable. I want it to feel—" he brings my hands to his lips and kisses my knuckles softly, making me shiver "—amazing. Spectacular. Best ever."

I swallow hard. "Best ever." My voice sounds far away to my ears.

Lips travel at intervals across my bare arms, over my shoulder, into the crook of my neck where he spends a long moment just breathing. Then the kissing starts up again, over my collarbone, dustings of kisses across my lips, along the curve of my ear. He keeps everything light, but the effect makes every place he touches tingle with anticipation. I'm surrounded by his warmth, his smell, his skin, his mouth, but I want more. He's holding himself back and I want him to lose control. I'm sick of being nervous, of waiting to screw up.

It's incredibly difficult, but I pull back because we're both a bit analytical and a clarification of terms might make us both feel better before we take the step that I think we're about to take.

"Hang on—please, wait."

He pauses immediately, waiting and watching me. His eyes are like aquamarine glass, and those damn lips, which have gotten me into all this trouble in the first place, are red from kissing me. I sway toward him involuntarily, then stop myself. "Okay, so you probably know I haven't done this in a while."

"Define a while."

I smile, because I knew he'd want data.

"Three years?" I make it a question because I sort of can't remember how long it's been. I remember the guy—Nico—and his apartment in Isla Vista. Grad school. I count back in my head. Yeah, a little over three years.

"But, I mean, it's pretty clear from your...toys, and what you said the other night, you're not, like, a nun." He has a tiny little blush on his cheeks and it's too adorable.

"Well, yeah. I mean, the last time I had sex with someone *else* was three years ago, but the last time I had an orgasm was this morning."

"Okay. Right. Me too." Then his blush intensifies and we both stare at each other. "TMI?" he asks. Then we're both laughing, tension broken.

"The point I'm trying to make," I say when we calm down, "is I'm super healthy, no diseases, but I'm not on birth control. So we should use a condom."

"I'm also clean. It's actually been a while for me, too."

"Oh yeah?"

"Since Kara."

"Kara? You guys broke up over a year ago."

"True."

"Wow."

"Why is that so hard to believe? You haven't had sex in three years."

"I know, but isn't it different for guys?"

"You know, some guys like to be in a relationship before they have sex."

I think about this. It doesn't surprise me that Jamie isn't into casual sex either. But does it scare me that we're embarking on an actual relationship here? Isn't this what I've been hiding from since...forever?

Jamie holds my gaze carefully. He seems tense, as if he

thinks maybe I'm going to walk. To push him away. To say this is all a mistake. And to be honest, a part of me wants to do that and go hide in my room and stay far away from this messiness.

What would Miss Rumphius do? She'd live. She'd grab hold of the adventure. She'd enjoy the beauty in front of her.

God, he's so beautiful.

"You have a condom?"

CHAPTER 24

JAMIE

I thank whatever instinct made me stash a couple of condoms in my wallet before coming over here tonight, because we're really doing this. We're in Ophelia's bedroom and by the soft glow of the bedside lamp she pulls me down on top of her and starts kissing the breath out of me.

Have you ever wanted something so badly—say, a cup of hot cocoa overflowing with marshmallows after spending the day skiing in freezing weather? Or to get your dream job that pays twice as much as your current gig? Or the sweet sporty car that you pass every day at the dealership on your way to work?

Having Ophelia in my arms, being with her not as friends but as lovers, is every want and need and desire I've ever had in my whole life wrapped into one. After thinking I would never have her, being with her like this is overwhelming. I almost can't believe it's happening.

I stop our kisses to trace my finger over her downy soft eyebrows, along the slope of her nose, her lips, her chin.

"Are you real?" I ask. I know I'm supposed to be keeping this light. But this is the woman I want to spend the rest of my life with. This is our first time and we'll remember it forever. I don't want to rush. I don't want to pretend it's casual.

"I'm real," Ophelia whispers. She closes her eyes and kisses me again, so soft, so sweet, and she arches into my touch, smoothing her hands over my back, my arms. She feels small against me, but she's not tentative, and thank fuck.

Ophelia's silky-smooth calves lead to her plump, firm thighs. My hands keep going up, up, up. I groan when my fingers brush over her panties and find them soaked through. "This dress is evil," I mumble, pushing it out of the way so I can get better access. There's so much I want to do, I barely know where to begin. But getting two fingers knuckle deep in her pussy seems like a good place to start. God, she's so wet, so ready, so fucking perfect.

"You don't like my dress?"

"It's been driving me crazy all night. Your legs. Jesus, fuck. Take it off." My tone sounds so harsh I tack on a "please" in a softer voice.

She giggles. "It's okay. I like it when you're a little bossy."

I raise my eyebrows. "Good to know."

She flops over onto her stomach, which exposes her barely covered ass. My fingers itch to grab it. But then she points to her zipper in silent instruction to undress her.

Taking all the time in the world is my stated mission, so I unzip the dress with agonizing slowness, practically hearing each tooth unbind. *Click, click, click.* Her back is smooth and creamy, dotted here and there with light brown moles. She's not wearing a bra. My mouth waters.

I lean over and kiss her everywhere I can reach, and she wriggles her arms out of the dress and sits up, letting it pool at her waist. She's bared herself to me, and I take a moment to simply look. Her hair's a mess, her lipstick long since worn off. Her breasts are full and sloped, the pink tips like cherries on the top of a rich scoop of French vanilla ice cream.

"May I?" I ask, gesturing toward them.

"Please," she says. The first taste is so good. She fits my

mouth exquisitely. I take my fill of her sweet and salty skin. Her hands are in my hair grasping and pulling and I'm afraid I'm going to come in my jeans from only my mouth on her.

"Um." I distantly register she's saying something. "Jamie. Can you…I mean, I need…"

I stop suckling her and rasp out a response. "Yeah?"

"Can you fuck me now?" she asks, so sweet, so…Ophelia.

"Yes, darling," I say. And then it's a matter of getting a condom out of my wallet, dropping my jeans to the floor and pulling my shirt over my head. She kicks off the dress and lies back on the bed in her underwear.

"There so much I want," I say, unable to be more eloquent. But she nods. She understands. There's going to be time for all of that. There has to be.

I roll her underwear down, and the inverted triangle of dark blonde curls between her legs is a visual I'll take to the grave. She's gorgeous. She's about to be mine.

There are a lot of pheromones flying around, and I'm sure that's influencing the tidal wave of affection I experience as I lie down beside her after I sheath myself in the condom. If I didn't think I'd be shooting myself in the foot and make her uncomfortable, I'd be saying, "I love you, Ophelia," before we take this step. Instead, I kiss her, long and slow.

"Ready?" I ask.

She nods. She kisses me. "Jamie—"

"Yeah?"

"I—I want you."

It's close. It's something. I swallow.

"I want you, too, Ophelia." And then her hands are on me, guiding me into her. It's tight, so tight, so warm. "Fuck."

"Uh huh," she gasps. I stop. Am I hurting her? She reads my mind: "No, it's okay, keep going."

She's slippery wet and I have no trouble sliding in up to the hilt. We adjust our positions until we find one that makes her cry out in pleasure. I need to give her that, I need her to feel that with me. I'm barely paying attention to how amazing this feels, because I'm watching her face, listening to her cries, feeling her writhe more and more feverishly as we move together, chasing satisfaction.

"Jamie!" It's that, my name on her lips, that brings me to a point I can't turn back from.

"O, I'm going to—"

"Yes," she cries, and she's tense all over, her nails digging into my arms. I'm lost now, plunging into her over and over, experiencing an orgasm more intense than I can remember.

She's still clinging to my arms, hard, when I come down enough from the high to register I'm on top of her, weighing her down. I roll to the side and we find a comfortable position facing each other. Her cheeks are flushed. She's not smiling, exactly, but at least she looks relaxed.

I don't want to be the clingy, needy one in our relationship —not that I want her to be clingy and needy. I don't want either of us to have to be clingy. Whatever.

I bite my tongue to stop from begging her for, if not a five-star review, then some kind of verbal feedback.

She tucks her face against my chest, and I use a tissue from the box on the bedside table to tuck away the condom for future disposal.

The longer the silence goes on, the closer to panicking I get. Oh God, she hated it. She hated having sex with me. Three years of celibacy and I blew it. She's never going to let me touch her again. This goes around my head on a loop for an endless minute before I hear a little snuffling sound.

Ophelia is crying. And it's all my fault.

"Jesus, sweetheart, don't cry. I'm sorry—we can have a do-over. We'll try something else. We'll work on it. I can do better."

"What are you talking about?" Her cheeks are wet and her eyes are puffy, but her voice sounds strong.

"I just—you're crying and—"

"I'm crying because sex does something perverse to girls' brains where pleasure makes them sad. I didn't know it could be like that. You made me feel—"

I hold my breath.

"—like, like a supernova, exploding and real and alive all at once. You made me feel the pain of absolute pleasure, knowing it's fleeting and it will be taken away at any second."

I cock my head and a lock of hair falls into my eyes. Ophelia brushes it away.

"So, you liked it then? The sex?" I sound completely stupid and I don't care.

Now she does smile and I think I might feel better even than when I came.

"I loved it."

"Then let's do it again."

"Okay."

CHAPTER 25

OPHELIA

S undays are usually my lazy day. I work hard for five days straight and then Saturday run around getting all my life shit together, and then on Sunday I give myself permission to do whatever I want. This usually consists of sleeping in, reading, and the occasional social engagement with either Jamie or Nicole, or sometimes Jamie *and* Nicole.

But this Sunday I have two unusual things fucking up my equilibrium. One is the brunch date I made with my dad in a fit of probably misguided theorizing that our relationship could stand to be warmed up by a couple degrees.

The other unusual thing is in my bed, flopped over on his stomach, head buried under a pillow, one arm cradling me gently around my middle. I'm lying on my side; all I can see of his naked body are the ridges of his shoulder blades and some tufts of black underarm hair smooshed against my sheets.

Something about that underarm hair makes me tingle. It's so male, so foreign in my cocoon of femininity. It reminds me that my nether-region is throbbing a bit from the enthusiastic workout it got the night before. I haven't been this sore after sex since...the first time I had sex.

I practically lost my virginity all over again last night. I knew what I was doing, in theory, having done it before. I knew the mechanics, anyway. But I was in no way prepared for how it would actually feel to have Jamie Kendell inside me. To have him kiss me and fuck me and treat me with both tenderness and outright carnality.

It felt good. To say the least.

The events of the night come back to me, one by one, like pictures in a very dirty slideshow. Our second bout of lovemaking, slower than the first but no less urgent. Stumbling half-naked back to the couch to ravenously consume the dinner we'd left half-finished. Putting the dishes in the sink until morning, dumping the caipis down the drain. We didn't need to drink. We were drunk on each other. Returning to bed, falling asleep with Jamie's breath warm on my neck and feeling oddly comforted by it instead of irritated.

Fucking fuck.

This was not in my plan. What right does he have to make me feel so good? It's completely backward to be annoyed by this, but I am. I thought I knew who I was and what I wanted. I thought I knew what I didn't want. I don't know who to be angry at. Him? Me? The world at large that makes us feel like being a part of a couple is the only way to be happy?

I sigh. It's not fair to make Jamie bear the brunt of my confusion just because he's there. To be more specific, he's *here*, in my bed, in my life. In my heart, now, deeper than he ever was before.

I flip over and when I see the time I sit up in shock. I'm supposed to meet my dad in an hour.

Jamie mumbles something from underneath the pillow and tries to grip my waist, but his arms and hands are floppy with sleep and he can't hang on as I slide out and head for the bathroom.

"I'm going to take a shower. Uh. You can go back to sleep?" I have no idea what I'm going to do about him, and my lateness gives me an excuse to put off figuring it out.

I lather my skin hastily. It feels different now that it has the knowledge of Jamie's body imprinted on it. It's overdramatic, but I feel fundamentally changed from the day before. Or maybe I'm the same girl I've always been, but with something extra. Maybe that's what a relationship in its best form gives you. You are yourself, only more so.

I finish washing, attempt to wrangle my hair into a knot. It's hopelessly tangled, and I'll have to condition the hell out of it later, but I don't have time now.

Jamie's awake and on his phone when I come back into the bedroom. He looks up at me, tosses his phone away, and curls his mouth into a smile. He looks young and cute and happy. I feel a stab of something in my general chest area. I think it's fear. I push away the suspicion that I'm going to hurt him sooner or later.

I have to get clothes from my overstuffed wardrobe on the other side of the bed. I debate whether or not to take them back into the bathroom to change. I don't feel shy, exactly, about dropping my towel and dressing in front of him, but I'm finding the transition between friends to lovers tricky. We slept together, but that doesn't mean I'm ready for real intimacy.

"I have to meet my dad. Sort of in a rush."

His smile fades marginally. "Oh, right. I forgot."

"Did I tell you?" I don't remember.

"No—he did, yesterday at breakfast club."

"Right." It's weird that Jamie sees my dad more than I do.

"Is it okay if I grab a quick shower here?"

"Sure. There's a towel in the cupboard." I watch, mouth dry, as he rises from the bed completely naked. I drink in his well-defined muscles, his flat stomach, his cock, half hard, bobbing in front of him. He seems completely at ease and for a minute I wonder how I got so lucky to have a guy who thinks like him and looks like him and fucks like him. If I'm even half as smart as I imagine myself to be, I'll do whatever I can not to screw this up.

Then I realize I'm staring and he's grinning and I blush. "Have a nice shower."

"Next time you should wait for me. Save water."

I've never shared a shower with another person. It sounds somewhat unhygienic and totally hot at the same time. "Okay. I have to get dressed. Shoo."

He's laughing as he closes the door behind him. I drop my towel and hold my hands up to my cheeks to cool their burning.

CHAPTER 26

OPHELIA

Even though Jamie's and my first sexual encounter wasn't exactly awkwardness-free, it was pretty outstanding. So I can't stop the little smile that creeps onto my face whenever I'm not paying attention. My dad notices it right away, to my utter chagrin.

"You look happy," he says as we wait for our table at the Biltmore. For some reason he wanted to meet up at one of the fanciest hotels in the city instead of his usual dive.

"Do I? You look happy, too," I deflect lamely.

He actually does. He's wearing a nicer version of his usual get-up in a nod to our surroundings: khakis and relatively unscuffed boat shoes, a crisp Hawaiian shirt under a tweed jacket. It doesn't make sense when you look at each part individually, but taken as a whole, my fifty-something dad looks pretty sharp. He's trimmer than the last time I saw him; his hair looks recently cut.

As a glossy hostess seats us, I get a sick feeling in my stomach. The location. The relative polish on my usually paint-stained, turpentine-soaked father.

"You're getting married again." It's not a question. I fiddle with my water glass instead of looking my father in the eye.

"Why would you say that? I'll have an iced tea, please."

"Same, please." I smile faintly at the server, but ignore my dad's question.

"Sweetie, I'm not getting married." Sheer relief has my stomach soaring the other way, leaving me faintly nauseated.

"But I am seeing someone. I'd like you to meet her, whenever works for you."

"Oh." This seems slightly more manageable. I look up. "What's her name?"

"Dakota."

"That's her first name?" I don't hide my skepticism.

"Yes, that's her first name. Her last name is Fisher."

"Only young people are named Dakota. Please tell me she's not younger than me."

He smiles. "She's seems young to me, but she's fifty-one. She's divorced, has a son in college at Santa Cruz. Let's see, she's an artist, like me."

I'm relieved to hear that she's not some high-powered thirty-year-old who's going to get tired of my dad's lack of drive the way Mom did. But it's hard to talk around the swirling in my gut. I know my dad has dated women in the years since he and Mom broke up, but he's never wanted to introduce me to any of them before.

"She sounds like a unicorn, Dad. Good for you."

"A unicorn?"

"A rare one. Someone to try and keep."

"Ah." He smiles—the expression seems to tickle him. "She is."

I want to be happy for him, but I've kept myself insulated from my dad's life for so long, being suddenly invested in his happiness, having him want something from me, is disconcerting.

"Maybe the three of us could have dinner sometime in the next few weeks?"

"Sure." That sounds vague enough to agree to.

"Or maybe we could go to the zoo? I haven't been there in ages."

I look up sharply. "The zoo?"

"You mentioning unicorns reminded me. You were about three and your mom and I took you there, and the whole time you kept asking us where the unicorn exhibit was. You were adorable."

I do remember being disappointed that they didn't have even one unicorn on hand. But I don't know if I can face going to the zoo with Dad and his new girlfriend. "Yeah, the zoo was always kind of yours and mine and Mom's thing."

We used to go every few months. Funny, I haven't been since their divorce. Lack of unicorns aside, I used to love the gentle grassy slopes and seeing my favorites over and over—the busily playing otters, the tranquil giraffes, the curious anteater. Going there with some lady my dad's sleeping with...ugh. I really do feel kind of sick.

"Just dinner, then," he says.

"Okay."

The server comes back around and Dad orders what sounds like a mountain of food.

"Um, I'll have a scone. And bacon."

"Breakfast of champions?" Dad says mildly.

"I don't feel very well."

"Oh, sweetie, do you want us to go?"

Yes. But I'm determined to see this through. "No, I'll be okay after I eat something."

"Rough night?"

Images of Jamie and me tangled up in my sheets flash through my brain. "Uh, not exactly."

"Tell me what's new with you. How's work?"

As I tell him about the latest programs we've been doing at the library, it occurs to me that he probably won't ask me about my personal life, because both he and my mother got the message years ago that there was nothing to report on that front and therefore no need to inquire.

I should be relieved. On the other hand, it feels strange not to tell him because he and Jamie see so much of each other. Am I going to ask Jamie to keep it a secret, too? Nicole and Kate know. And let's be honest, everyone else who was at the party the night we hooked up knows.

My dad's digging into his meal and I'm picking at a piece of bacon when I decide it would be weirder to say nothing and have him find out from someone else.

"I do have some news."

"Oh?"

"You know Jamie? Kendell? Ricky's cousin."

He gives me a quizzical look. "Of course. I saw him yesterday."

"Right. It turns out—" I stop. How do I even explain our relationship? "You know that we're good friends."

"I do."

"So I don't know where it's going—" *Liar*, my brain supplies. *It's going to end badly.* "—but we're dating now."

"You and Jamie? Together?" He seems genuinely surprised. I hope it's because I'm dating period, not Jamie specifically.

"Don't make a big thing of it," I add. Not that my dad makes a big thing of anything.

"Okay."

Then nothing. Is it any wonder I have trouble expressing my feelings?

"Don't you have an opinion?"

"Do you want it?"

"I guess."

"I think Jamie's a fine man and I hope you'll be very happy together."

"That's it?"

He sighs, and I can see him summoning the energy to dig deep and give me a better answer. "Look, Ophelia, I know Jamie. He's very passionate. He cares deeply. If he has feelings for you, they're probably serious feelings. And I know you have had some trouble connecting with people since your mom and I split up. I don't want either of you to get hurt."

I can't believe what I'm hearing. My dad is baring my worst fears in the dining room at the Biltmore. I had no idea he was so perceptive, or that I was so transparent. It's hard to take.

"And whose fault is that!" My volume rises, along with my resentment. I glance around, hoping no one is paying attention to my mini meltdown. "What you're saying is I can't return his feelings, so I shouldn't mess with him? That I'm going to use him and then break his heart? Is that what you really think of me?"

"Of course not. I didn't mean that at all. If you care about him—"

"Of course I care about him. I'm not a robot." Jesus. Even my own father thinks I'm going to mess this up.

"Do you love him? Because he'd be a chump not to love you. And if you guys are in this together, all the way, then this could be it for you. No one would be happier than me. But if you're trying this on, ready to send him back if it gets hard, then you better tell him now and save a lot of heartache. Believe me, if your mother—"

He stops, but I need to know what he's not telling me.

"What about Mom?"

"I wanted to make it work. I tried being someone I wasn't. Your mom tried, too, for a while. But it wasn't in her. I wasn't what she wanted. Our life wasn't the one she wanted."

I never thought of myself as more like my mom than my dad when it came to love. She had dreams and plans and the ability to pull them off. I have dreams and plans, too. And they never involved a man with sinful lips, dreamy eyes, a garage full of tools, a huge...*brain*. A huge heart, too. He's given me so much room to be myself, so much support.

Is it possible for me to have the life I want and the man I want, too?

I'm quiet for a long time and when I look back at Dad he's busily finishing his omelet. Emotions apparently don't affect his appetite the way they affect mine.

"A relationship needs more than attraction or even love to work," he says gently. "There's got to be some basic agreement over the shape of your lives. Otherwise everything will be out of whack."

The thing is, Jamie and I had an agreement. We were friends who didn't talk about relationships and everything was fine. More than fine. Except now I know it wasn't. He wanted me, and I repressed any knowledge of it. We weren't being honest.

Maybe we still aren't, if we think this is going to be easy.

"Thanks, Dad," I say eventually.

"For what?"

"For telling me what I need to hear, even if I don't want to hear it. I think back then..." I swallow. Why is this so hard to talk about, even ten years later? "...I couldn't hear you and Mom, when you told me things were changing, and why they were changing. I didn't want it to happen and I didn't listen. I only thought about myself."

"Natural for a teenager."

"Yeah, but I wish I hadn't been so hard on you guys. You tried, I know you did."

"I should've tried harder to keep you in my life. I let you slip away. It's my greatest regret."

"Really?"

"Of course. You're my family. My baby girl."

Shit. I'm going to cry. I blink hard, but it doesn't help. Dad sees my tears and his eyes start to well up, which makes me go even harder.

"Dad, stop."

"I want you to know how much I love you. I don't say it enough."

"Of course I know that, you big softie."

He dabs his eyes. "Who are you calling a softie, softie?"

"You! And pass me my scone."

My appetite seems to have returned.

CHAPTER 27

JAMIE

When Ophelia goes off to meet Andy, I head straight for my workshop. I have a lot of work to do on my printer prototype. All week, my brain wouldn't stop interrupting my productivity with crystal-clear high-resolution images of the way Ophelia looks right before I kiss her—ripe and expectant—or right after I kiss her—moist and lovely. Now that we've had sex, I'm having a hard time thinking about anything other than the sensation of her body underneath mine.

I'm irritated with myself. I'm twenty-seven. I've had plenty of sex before. I shouldn't be so distracted by this.

But being with her was as brain-meltingly hot as I'd suspected it would be. I'm more convinced than ever that we should be together, now and always. But it feels like the tighter I try to hold onto that, the faster she'll slip away from me.

Knowing what I do about her family, I can't blame her for being skittish. But it doesn't do much for my pride to know that she's willing to sleep with me but not willing to really let me in, to really be her partner. I'm ready to do this, to be together, one hundred percent. I can easily imagine her moving in with me someday soon. There's plenty of room in my two-bedroom.

Not that my suggesting we move in together wouldn't be the worst possible idea.

I sigh and slam my goggles up over my forehead. I'm not getting anywhere. I keep checking my phone to see if Ophelia's texted me. She's probably still at brunch.

So I'm surprised when I check again and there is a text. Not from Ophelia, though. It's from my mom.

MOM

I need you to go to Lilac and pick up dessert

For a minute I have no idea what she's talking about. I'm so out of it, I forgot I said I'd go to my parents' for dinner tonight. My mom and dad and I all have a sweet tooth, but none of us can bake to save our lives, so we're connoisseurs of every treat-producing establishment in the greater Santa Barbara area. Even gluten-free ones, like Lilac. Hey, good cake is good cake.

On it. Carrot cake?

Whatever looks good

I miss Ophelia. Bring her if she's free.

I frown. Ophelia and my parents get along like a house on fire, and she's always welcome at family gatherings. But tonight might be too soon. Too much. It's frustrating that I have to be so careful, always worried about putting too much pressure on this nascent relationship.

Still, I can't be walking on eggshells all the time, or this is never going to work.

I'll see if she can make it.

I'm about to text Ophelia when I realize I can improve my printer's extrusion power by reprogramming a few things, and when I next look up, a few hours have passed. I grab my phone, worried that I've missed a call from Ophelia, but there's nothing.

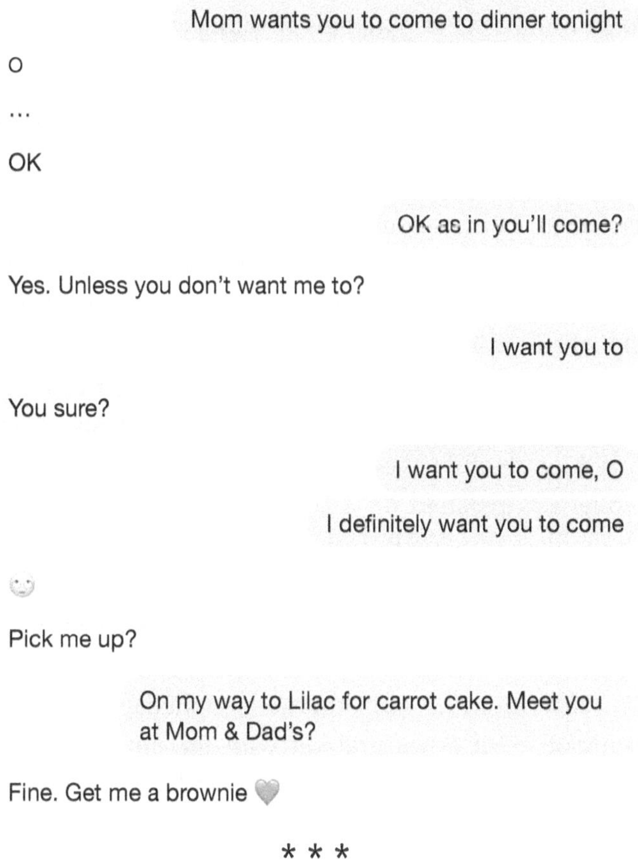

* * *

My parents have always taken an intense approach with my girlfriends. They vet her to make sure their only child isn't going to saddle them with a nightmare of a daughter-in-law, and if she passes their initial tests, they do their best to make her like them more than me, so she'll want to do girly things with my poor daughter-deprived mom and listen to all my dad's super-embarrassing stories about my adolescence.

After Kara moved, Ophelia sort of slipped into the vacant girlfriend role, coming with me to family dinners, showing my mom how to find stuff at the vintage shops in town, arguing with my dad about who's the greater writer, Madeleine L'Engle or Roald Dahl. They're both fans of young adult classics.

Mom and Dad have never once intimated that Ophelia should be more than a friend. She's their nephew's fiancée's cousin, for heaven's sake. They know as well as anyone that Ophelia is simply part of the family.

Will they think it's cool or weird that we've blurred the lines in our relationship?

Only one way to find out.

Ophelia's car is parked behind my mom's ancient Mercedes wagon in the driveway, so I park on the street in front of the two-story ranch-style house I grew up in. I let myself in the kitchen door, careful to keep my precious cargo steady.

Ophelia is perched on a stool at the bar in the kitchen. There's a glass of wine in front of her, and my dad is pulling ribs out of the oven. The air is thick with spices and my stomach rumbles. A wave of contentment washes over me, so powerful that I have to stop for a moment and remind myself this is real. Until I'm told otherwise, Ophelia is my girl and we're about to sit down and eat with my other two favorite people in the world. How did I get so lucky?

"What are you standing there for? Put that cake on ice and help me get these ribs on the table," Dad says.

I drop the bag with the brownie in front of Ophelia and stick the cake in the fridge.

"What's that?" Mom asks, eying Ophelia's bag as she comes into the kitchen and gives me a hello hug.

"Something for later," I say, winking at Ophelia. She smiles shyly, and all my certainty evaporates. If things were different, I'd be going to stand close to her, put my hand at the small of her back, kiss her hello. After two years of having

Ophelia at arm's distance, I'm anxious to make up for lost time.

But something in her expression stops me and I'm stuck in limbo. We have to tell them sometime, right? Unless this is all going to collapse and get labeled some surreal phase of our friendship. Fuck. I hate this waiting and watching and wondering if my next move will be the one that finishes things.

My dad, oblivious to my turmoil, hands me a knife and nods at the ribs, so I sidestep Ophelia and set to splitting up the tender meat into portions. The conversation flows around me. I've apparently come in the middle of a story O's telling about work.

"The book fair throws my whole routine out of whack, but it's worth it. The kids get so excited, and the parents are great about volunteering, so even though it's crazy, it's fun. And it's helpful for me to see what's flying off the shelves. Superheroes and anything mermaid-related are very popular right now."

"Mermaids, really?" Mom asks.

"They're the new unicorns. Or maybe the new dolphins," Ophelia confirms.

"What I missed out on by having a boy." My mom shakes her head. "It was all robots and dinosaurs and spaceships around here."

I grin. I was a pretty typical boy. Except I never got bored of the robots and spaceships, started building versions of my own, and I haven't stopped.

"Good thing you have Ophelia for doing girly stuff."

"And what is this girly stuff you think we do?" Ophelia asks pertly.

I know it's a trap, but I play along. "Oh, painting your nails and shopping. Glitter. Pink stuff."

"You know, he's right, Laura," Ophelia says, turning to Mom. "We totally haven't gone shopping for pink glitter nail polish in forever. Let's get that on the calendar right now."

Mom laughs. "It sounds like you'll be too busy to go shopping for a while. Jamie was telling me about some of your ideas for expanding the maker lab program. It sounds fabulous."

Ophelia flicks me a glance. "Yeah, it's a solid idea."

The ribs are fragrant and my stomach is growling, so I listen while helping my dad bring the food out. Mom grabs the wine and Ophelia transfers our glasses to the table, setting hers down at the place next to mine.

"I saw Mihret at a fundraiser a couple of days ago and she told me she wanted you to head the whole initiative. What a fantastic opportunity. You know, if you ever want to jump ship from schools to museums full time, I'm sure between Mihret and me we could find you a position that would tap into all your skills."

Ophelia laughs, a bit forced. "Thanks for saying that, but I still love my job. Maybe in a few years the kids will drive me bonkers enough to want a change. Plus, I'm still waiting to hear about the librarian exchange fellowship I applied for."

"Don't take this the wrong way when I tell you I kind of hope you don't get it. We would hate for you to be so far away for so long." My dad says what I've been thinking every day since Ophelia told me she applied.

I take a bite of food, not tasting it. When it comes to Ophelia and me, I wish I could micromanage everything like I do when I'm designing a program or building a new printer. But there's no way to control all the outcomes. Maybe Ophelia will leave me to go to Newfoundland or Ethiopia or wherever that fellowship will send her. Or maybe she'll give up on trying to make us work once the novelty of us sleeping together wears off. Suddenly, breaking the news to my parents that we're together doesn't seem like the best idea.

"What's new with you, Jamie?" Dad asks, as if suddenly remembering I'm here, too.

"Uh." I glance at Ophelia. She won't meet my eyes. Maybe

she's scared I'm going to out our relationship. Maybe we should have talked about this before it got to this point.

"Testing is going great on the new printer design. Ricky's helping me line up a few companies to take a look at it. So that's good."

"And how about wedding stuff?" Mom asks.

I have a moment of cognitive dissonance where I think in some version of this universe she's talking about Ophelia's and my wedding. I've got to get my head on straight.

I guess I'm silent for too long, because Ophelia answers, "Nicole's got everything well in hand. The next big thing is the bachelorette weekend."

"I didn't have a bachelorette party before I married Rory," Mom says. "My sister and a couple girlfriends took me out for cocktails the night before, but I didn't have any ID, so they had to order at the bar and sneak me shots. We were so young."

"How young?"

"I was twenty. Rory was twenty-three. We were dumb kids. But I guess it's worked out pretty well," she says, giving Dad a fond look.

"Wow," Ophelia says softly. "I didn't realize that."

"Yeah, we waited a long time before trying for kids, and then it took a while to get pregnant. But I'm happy we were together for so long before having a kid. This one," she nods at me, "was pretty great, but it turns your life upside down."

"I can't even imagine," Ophelia says with feeling. I wonder. She's never indicated that she wants to have children. Does that matter?

I'm full of questions and anxiety and my parents won't stop talking about marriage and children. My chair's legs scrape noisily against the Mexican tile floor as I escape from the table.

"I forgot something in my car. Be right back."

My parents aren't fazed. They keep eating, and my mom

muses about what to get Nicole and Ricky for their wedding present.

I glance at Ophelia. She doesn't seem aware of my acute anxiety, but also, she doesn't seem her usual cool-as-a-cucumber self.

"Help me, Ophelia?" It's both a question and a literal cry for help.

"Uh, sure." She gets up and as we head back through the kitchen door, it feels like we're breaking out of a high-security prison. I stalk to my car.

"What is going on?" Ophelia asks, hurrying behind me. "Why are you being so weird?"

"I'll tell you, but first—" I close my lips over hers, wrapping my arms around her soft curves. She melts into me, and I lose myself in the kiss. I hadn't realized how badly I wanted—or needed—to do that.

After a minute we pull our mouths and bodies apart but stay close. I need to be near her, in her orbit.

"I'm sorry," I say.

"For what?"

"I should have prepared better for this. We need to talk about what we're going to tell them."

"You didn't tell them?" She looks at me strangely.

"No—why? Did you?"

"No! I thought the whole point of inviting me to dinner was because they knew and wanted to include me. And then you barely said hello to me when you got here and I got super confused and—"

"Jesus fuck. I'm sorry. I'm not usually this much of a mess when it comes to dating."

"Yeah, you're one smooth operator."

I deserve the dry-as-dust tone she throws at me.

"You know me. Mr. Smooth."

"Then I guess I'm special, huh? Mixing you all up?" She puts a hand on her hip and cocks it out dramatically.

"Ophelia, you are special." I can't help reaching out to touch her again. "You're my kryptonite, apparently."

"That sounds like it could be a problem. Doesn't that make Superman...impotent?" She quirks her lips. Vixen.

"That's a bad analogy. I just mean we're the same, but everything is different. And I like it, but I'm terrified that I'm going to do something to screw it up."

"You're terrified *you're* going to screw it up? That's my wheelhouse, buddy. Get in line for the self-doubt, I've got a monopoly on it." Her tone is teasing, but I can tell she's not really joking. She's as scared as I am. Maybe that's a good thing. Maybe it means we're both serious about making this work, even if we're not convinced it can.

"We're a pair of dorks," I say.

Ophelia tips her head up, and I take it as an invitation to kiss her senseless. "Two of a kind," she whispers against my mouth.

"Well." My mother's voice from the foot of the driveway makes me jerk away from Ophelia like I'm twelve and caught sneaking candy before dinner. "That explains what's taking you two so long."

CHAPTER 28

OPHELIA

"House. Now." Jamie's mother doesn't sound particularly happy, and I can't bring myself to look her in the eye as Jamie releases me. Laura walks back up the drive, not waiting to see if we'll follow.

"Did your mom see us kissing?"

"I'm pretty sure she saw my hand on your boob, too."

"Ugh. Are you trying to be funny right now?"

"Not really." He sighs. "Let's just go tell them the truth."

"Which is?"

Jamie faces me, his rueful smile gone. "Why don't you tell me? I don't want to be the one defining things all the time."

I'm stung, but he's right. I'm playing it safe and it's not fair. If the conversation with my dad this morning taught me anything, it's that Jamie would rather die than hurt me, and I've got to trust in this enough to give it a real shot. I think back to Miss Rumphius and straighten my spine.

"You're right. I've got this." I sense Jamie's surprise, but he doesn't speak.

Laura and Rory are talking in hushed tones when we get back to the house. I slip Jamie's hand into mine and Rory's eyebrows shoot up an inch or two. They must really not have seen this coming.

To be fair, neither did I.

"Believe it or not, Jamie and I are dating," I say, my voice steady. That wasn't so hard. It's the second time I've said it today. Maybe I'm getting used to the idea. I squeeze Jamie's hand and he squeezes mine back reassuringly.

"That's it?" Laura's voice gives nothing away.

"Um…" I could elaborate by saying we're having sex, but I think it's implied, and while Laura and I are close, we aren't *that* close. "…yeah?"

"You've been in each other's pockets for two years and all of a sudden you're 'dating?' Isn't that kind of an antiseptic word?"

"Mom." Jamie's voice is sharp. "What else do you want us to say? It's new. We realized that we have feelings for each other. Don't make it a big thing."

"But it is a big thing! You guys are cousins-in-law. Don't you think—" Laura stops herself. I'm surprised she's being this negative. I thought on some level they'd be happy; they already treat me like a daughter. But perhaps they have the same reservations as my dad. He was being honest when he warned me not to screw around with Jamie's heart. His parents would probably want to warn me of that ten times over. "I want to be sure you are thinking this through."

"Mom," Jamie starts, but I put a hand on his arm to stop him.

"Laura. I understand where you are coming from. You have concerns. But this isn't a game to us. We wouldn't be exploring this if we didn't think there was something…real…between us." It's as close as I've come to admitting that my feelings for Jamie can't be brushed aside or explained away by temporary insanity.

Laura's worried look doesn't exactly go away, but she doesn't say anything, and Rory steps in, as if they'd rehearsed it: good parent/worried parent.

"We wish you all the best," Rory says. "Really. Jamie would be lucky to hang onto a girl like you, Ophelia."

I smile. "Thank you."

"Of course. We adore you, sweetheart," Laura says, as if realizing she'd strayed too deep into mama bear mode. "It's just that we never thought—you never seemed—Jamie didn't—" She smiles self-deprecatingly at her aborted attempts to explain.

"Jamie didn't seem into me, and I didn't seem into anyone," I say, trying to be helpful.

"Pretty much."

"Yeah, about that," Jamie says. He looks at me, and there's a glint in his eyes that has my cheeks instantly burning. I feel a stab of want that's almost painful. God, he's so freaking cute. I want to run my fingers through that mop of hair and kiss him until the only thing he can think of are my lips, my body, my name. "I'm into her."

"That has made itself manifest," Rory says, chuckling. I pull myself back to the present. We're still in his parents' dining room. Not the place to get all gooey and bothered.

"Let's have a piece of that cake. I need sugar," Laura says briskly.

Skipping to dessert and getting out of there as quickly as possible seems like a very good idea indeed.

* * *

Dessert seems to normalize things, and by the time we leave Laura and I have a lunch date for the following weekend, and Jamie and his dad are talking about some modifications Jamie wants to do on his car. We don't kiss or hold hands or anything on our way out, but I can't miss the way his parents watch us carefully as we leave together. Jamie remembers to grab the brownie he bought for me and I stash it in my bag.

When we're out of earshot, Jamie says, "That could have gone worse, I guess."

"Next time we need to plan ahead."

"Definitely."

"So, what are you doing now?" I ask.

"That depends. I'm either going home with you or you're going home with me. Take your pick."

"It's a school night," I say halfheartedly. "I really shouldn't."

"Yeah, you should."

Since the only thing I want is to feel his body on top of mine, I can't argue. I debate. If we go to his house, I won't have any of my things, but I'll be able to leave whenever I want. If he comes over, I'll have my stuff but I won't be able to kick him out and have my alone time.

"Come over," I say finally. "But we have work in the morning, so maybe you shouldn't stay over."

"Let's play it by ear."

If this is going to be a regular thing, it would be so much easier if we were in the same place. Easier, but way more intense. I don't even know if I'm going to be in Santa Barbara in six months. I shouldn't be thinking about moving in with someone.

We arrive at my place almost simultaneously and don't make it two steps through the front door before we're tearing each other's clothes off. It hasn't been that long since we had sex, but the fact that we're allowed to do this now is enough to make me hot and achy and desperate to feel his body against mine.

We don't waste time on words as we shed a trail of clothes to the bedroom. We fall on cool sheets, my skin humid-hot, especially everywhere he touches me. All I'm wearing is my bra and underwear. Jamie's in boxers, still wearing his glasses. I happen to think he looks sexier with them on, the way they frame his sea green eyes, but they can get in the way when we kiss, so he takes a moment to remove them and set them carefully on the bedside table.

"Am I blurry now?" I ask, when he comes back to my side.

"Like looking at a Monet from a foot away," he answers, then starts kissing my shoulder, slipping my bra straps down, fondling my nipples through the fabric, and it doesn't matter how anything looks, only how it feels. I'm shaking like a rocket hurtling through the atmosphere, ready to break apart as the pressure builds inside me.

I wrap my legs around his waist and he rubs his erection against the vee of my sex. My head lolls back; I'm too over-whelmed to do much besides respond to the onslaught of kisses and caresses. Someday I'll be the one in charge. I'll make him desperate for me and I'll make him feel so good he won't be able to remember his name.

But right now I'm the one who's desperate for relief. I can't even wait to take off my underwear. I pull down his boxers, his cock springing hard into my palm, then push aside my panties as I guide him to my entrance.

"Ophelia—condom," Jamie says, his voice ragged. Oh shit. I completely forgot, that's how far gone I am. I yank open my bedside table drawer and throw the box at him.

"Hurry."

He tears at the package like a starving animal and only a few seconds pass before he's pressing into me excruciatingly slowly. I'm practically sobbing underneath him, trying to get more friction, scrambling to get closer to my release.

"Jesus fuck, O, you are so tight." He pants, then stills once he's all the way inside me.

"Please move." I can't be bothered not to beg. I need this, I need to feel him inside me, all around me. "Just do it."

He obeys with a snap of his hips and I cry out on every

thrust. I'm coming, and I keep coming, and he's not even touching my clit. We're connected at one vital point, and I feel it everywhere. "Jamie, Jamie," I chant. "Don't stop."

"If I don't stop I'm going to—"

"Yes, yes." I don't care.

I ride the wave of my orgasm, and still he's not through pounding into me.

"Ophelia, I—"

"Yes, yes," I say again. I want him to know how good it is, how much he's giving me what I want. I want him to experience the same explosion of pleasure he's given me. "Jamie, please."

Then he groans and I feel another spasm inside me. He's coming and it seems to go on and on the way mine did. Eventually he collapses to my side, his lips latching onto mine for a deep, hard, slow kiss—the whipped cream on top of everything else. He's addictive, and I'm beginning to think I won't be able to live without this.

CHAPTER 29

Good news! Got my Rx filled. We can have condomless sex soon!

Is this an April Fool's joke?

haha I totally forgot that's today. No, for realsies

Then that is good news

Dinner later?

Sure. I have lots of leftover BBQ. Want to stay over?

It's a weeknight

Oh right I forgot. No sleepovers on weeknights

Them's the rules

BTW, I have to go to LA next weekend for some meetings

Meetings on the weekend?

They're working around my museum schedule.
I was thinking you could come down with me
Friday, we could stay somewhere nice, come
back Sunday?

It'll be the last couple days of your spring
break

> I don't know—the bachelorette is the weekend
> after

It's just one weekend

We could go to the Arclight

> Tempting

You know what Oscar Wilde said

> He said a lot of things

The only way to get rid of a temptation is to
yield to it

> Paraphrasing

I think he was right

> I'll think about it

* * *

Never a Bride(smaids)

OPHELIA

> So you gals need me to do anything for the
> bachelorette? Specifically the weekend before.
> Like, anything urgent that can't happen any
> other time???

KATE

Rosie & I have everything covered. But thanks for the weirdly specific offer

No problem

ROSIE

What's going on, O?

Nothing

Jamie asked me to go with him to LA that weekend

ROSIE

And you're looking for a reason not to go?

LANI

If you don't want to go, tell him no. He'll deal

KATE

How did he ask you?

Text

KATE

No, like how did he frame it, my literal-minded friend. As like a romantic mini-break or something else?

Oh. He has some work meetings & said I could come with & we'd do stuff together

LANI

Not exactly a red carpet invitation

ROSIE

Maybe he didn't want to pressure you, so he's keeping it casual

KATE

Are things still casual between you two?

I mean, we see each other almost every day &
we sleep over at each other's places every
weekend

LANI

Except for the sleepovers that doesn't sound
different from before

It's not. We're still best friends.

LANI

You realize you're doing it, O. Living the dream
—many have attempted, few have achieved.

???

LANI

Friends with benefits! It was an urban myth but
no longer—you and Jamie are proof

Haha I guess

KATE

So what's the harm in going away for the
weekend?

ROSIE

You'll probably have tons of fun. Gus and I
spent last Sunday at the Huntington Garden.
Spectacular.

I guess it's not a big deal

LANI

Only go if you want to, not because he wants
you to.

Thanks for the advice, ladies. You're the best.

ROSIE

Any time

KATE

LANI

Never a Bride(smaids) stick together 😄

* * *

OPHELIA

I'm in for LA

JAMIE

Rad. I'll get the hotel

OK

Should I plan anything?

I'll take care of everything. You're in charge of
driving music

You sure you want to give me that much
power?

I trust you

Famous last words

Seriously, O, this is going to be great

Great

CHAPTER 30
OPHELIA

"So I'll text you when I'm done." Jamie hovers over the open passenger door.

"Got it. Have a good meeting." My send-off is cursory as I'm parked in a loading zone and don't want to get a ticket. I hate driving in L.A. "Go."

Jamie winks at me and shuts the door. I check my mirrors and pull out of the illegal parking space with relief. I've been jittery all morning, but now I have two hours to myself and I'm going to enjoy it. Even though I'm technically on spring break, part of me still feels like I'm playing hooky from work. It's a gorgeous day, so I try to elevate my mood to fit my surroundings.

It's not that I'm not excited to spend a weekend with my boyfriend, but I'm intimidated by the implications. This is a big deal for us. For me. I'm still getting used to the idea that I even have a boyfriend. The longer we're together, the less casual this gets, and the more heartbroken he—I—*we'll* be when things go downhill.

I drive a few blocks and park at the Promenade—block after block of restaurants and shops all under the aquamarine Santa Monica sky. I've got to get over myself. Jamie deserves a girlfriend who can do stuff like this—a simple weekend away—without complicating things with an identity crisis.

I browse, but the chain clothing stores hold no appeal since I acquire most of my wardrobe from consignment and vintage shops. Then I stumble on a European-style lingerie shop and perk up. Even I don't wear secondhand underwear. The boutique is full of pastel scraps of lace and I find myself drawn to a blue bra and panty set the exact shade of the sky outside. Thirty minutes later I have a shopping bag full of pretty lacy things that I think Jamie will enjoy as much as I will, or, to be honest, probably more.

I buy an iced tea and settle on a stool in the window of the coffee shop so I can people watch without getting a sunburn. Maybe I'll get a hat while I'm in shopping mode. I place my phone on the counter so I won't miss Jamie's text and notice I have new emails. I shouldn't look—it's not a workday for me—but I can't help myself. I scroll through my inbox and one message pops out at me. It's from the nonprofit that administers the fellowship I applied for months ago.

> Dear Ms. Winesap,
> Thank you for your interest in the program. We have filled all spaces for the upcoming rotation and invite you to reapply next term.

Etc. Etc.

I didn't get it. The initial stab of rejection fades after a minute. I always knew it was a long shot. I had a strong application, but still, they only offer five slots a year.

I close the app and stare out the window at the tourists and high schoolers and families parading in front of me. For some reason not getting it doesn't feel as bad as it should. Instead, I'm sort of relieved I won't have to negotiate a leave of absence from my job and sublet my place and tell Jamie that I'm going to live abroad for a year.

He knows I applied, but we never talked about what it would mean for us if I got it, just one of the things we carefully don't talk about. Now the decision has been made for me. I'll stay home and everything can stay the same. Nicole won't have to do without me. I can see the maker lab project through to completion. I can still make a difference in Santa Barbara. And Jamie and I will still have each other.

I'm happy—at peace, even. It's okay to still be in the librarian phase of my Miss Rumphius life plan. I'll go on my world tour someday. I have time to figure out how to make the world a more beautiful place. Besides, I live in my own kind of paradise. I even have someone to share it with.

But even though I'm not disappointed to be rejected, I'm a bit dissatisfied with myself that I'm not more upset. Shouldn't I be reaching for the stars? Not letting anything hold me back? My contradictions make me sulky. I'm content with what I have, but maybe I shouldn't be.

My shopping-induced good cheer has worn off by the time I meet back up with Jamie. He seems charged up from his meeting and tells me to switch seats with him, which rubs my already prickly skin the wrong way.

"You've done enough driving today, babe," he says.

"I'm fine."

"You hate driving in the city. Don't worry about it."

"It's not my favorite thing but I can do it."

"I know you can do it. I thought maybe you'd like a break."

Why am I being contrary? I do want a break. He's just so freaking gallant all the time. It's annoying. Everything is annoying me since I got that email and realized that I'm actually happy I didn't get the fellowship.

"Fine." I slam the car into park and tear open my door, not looking at him as I round the hood to the passenger side.

"Is something wrong?" he asks with the sort of trepidatious tone of savvy boyfriends whose girlfriends are in bitch mode for some unknown reason that probably relates to them.

When I don't answer right away, because there is something wrong but I can't quite verbalize what it is, he goes on. "Did something happen while I was in my meeting?"

Yes, something happened. I didn't get the fellowship, which means we don't have to break up, and I don't have to make any hard decisions about my life, and I'm ambivalent about my ambivalence about not getting in.

Saying that would be too real for me to handle on this sunny spring day. I think about my recently purchased lingerie and about the fact that Jamie has planned this whole weekend for us and I don't want to ruin it. So I lie.

"Nothing's wrong. Sorry. I think I need to eat something." I smile and kiss him on the cheek by way of apology. He gives me a long look, as if he doesn't completely buy it, but he doesn't prod. Instead, he pulls into traffic and I settle back in my seat.

It's a relief not to be driving anymore. I don't know why I made such a big deal of it. *Because you're a terrible girlfriend?* I can't help but accuse myself.

Then again, would a terrible girlfriend drop two hundred dollars on underwear expressly designed to drive her boyfriend crazy?

Good point.

I give myself a pass.

"I'm starving, too. What do you think? Burgers or sushi?"

"Both."

CHAPTER 31

JAMIE

When we're stuffed with both burgers and sushi and a shared vanilla milkshake to fill in the cracks, Ophelia seems less stroppy. I guess she had low blood sugar or something.

We blast The Kinks and inch our way across town on the jam-packed 10 Freeway. Apparently everyone in Los Angeles wants to be somewhere else on a Friday afternoon.

We're headed to a spot I discovered last time I was downtown for the maker conference way back in January. I've wanted to bring Ophelia there ever since. I have a sneaking suspicion she'll love it.

I hope so, anyway.

There's something invisible pressing down on this weekend, distorting our simple getaway into something bigger. I've become obsessed with making it perfect for O. If I can show her how great we are as a couple, how we can have it all—romance, fun, sex—then maybe I can relax.

I've been trying to enjoy each moment I have with Ophelia, but every day that I don't tell her exactly how I feel about her feels something like a lie.

How long will it be before I can't do it anymore?

I fork over fifteen bucks to park around the corner from our destination.

"Will you finally tell me where we're going?"

"Give me thirty more seconds," I say, leading her around the corner of 5th Street and right up to the plate glass window.

"It's a bookstore!" she exclaims.

"The Last Bookstore," I confirm. The dramatic name of the store is kind of fitting. The ground floor is a huge room filled with wooden shelves of books, plus records and other analog-type stuff. The part that Ophelia's going to flip over is upstairs.

"This place is incredible." The smile on her face is that of a true bibliophile. I've brought her to a place where she can mainline her favorite drug—books.

"There's more." I guide her to the stairs and she follows me uncharacteristically obediently. When we get to the second floor, she laughs with delight. There are even more books up here, rows and rows and rooms and rooms and piles and piles of used books. Her eyes grow round.

"Um. Can I live here?"

"You sure can. Until about six-thirty, because we have reservations."

"I'll take it." She laughs again, and my heart swells because she's so obviously thrilled.

We spend a while browsing. Neither of us needs more books, but that's not the point. She squeals over finding an old-school Nancy Drew hardcover that she doesn't have, and I salivate over some architecture books I've never seen before. We browse together, occasionally brushing hands and twining our fingers together, until one or the other of us is drawn to pull another book off the shelf. Pretty soon Ophelia's arms are full. I offer to carry her haul for her.

"This is the best," she says, as she loads me up with novels and cookbooks. I think she has more cookbooks than utensils to actually cook with. "Thank you for thinking of it."

Unexpectedly, she kisses me, warm, tender. If we didn't have twenty pounds of books sliding between our arms I would wrap myself around her and never want to let go.

"You're welcome," I whisper.

She smiles, kind of shyly, but shining with joy. Suddenly, the effort of holding my feelings inside is too much. "Ophelia, I—"

"Look." She points to the other end of the landing, where a crowd has gathered to look over the side and down onto the ground floor. I follow behind her helplessly as she goes to see what's going on.

Below us is an unmistakable scene. A crowd forms a loose circle around a man on bended knee while a woman looks on, her hands clasped over her mouth, looking blissfully over-whelmed.

"Jasmine Adele Pandacharya, you are the love of my life and I want to spend every day from now until forever making you happy. Will you marry me?" Maybe the guy is an actor because his voice carries all the way to the nosebleed section.

The crowd cheers as the shocked woman nods, clearly crying, and I can't help the sympathetic tear that springs to my own eye.

Wearing a face-splitting grin, the guy puts a ring on her finger and sweeps her up in a good old-fashioned Hollywood kiss while the crowd whoops and hollers around them. I'd clap if I had my hands free, so I let out an approving whistle.

Nothing like a romantic gesture to make our ordinary date seem extraordinary. I turn to Ophelia to compare notes, but her face looks like she's tasted something sour.

"Ugh. That was so cliché," she says.

Ophelia's curmudgeonly attitude immediately pops my balloon. "What? Come on, that was awesome."

"Are you serious? The public proposal, the getting down on one knee. Of course she had to say yes. What if she was only doing it to save herself the embarrassment of turning him down in public?"

I peer back down where the newly-affianced couple is accepting congratulations from random strangers. Both of them are positively glowing. "I don't think so. They look pretty goddamned happy to me."

"Maybe. I think you've got to be selfish to do that in front of all those people."

"I think he wants to show her how much he loves her."

"Whatever. It's embarrassing."

"I think it's romantic." I should probably let this go, but I can't help being grouchy. Because what those two people down there have—not necessarily the public proposal, but the unbridled, unrestrained commitment to each other—I want that. I want Ophelia to want that, too. And I don't know what it means for us if we're never going to want the same thing.

CHAPTER 32

OPHELIA

"So what are our reservations?" I ask as we ride the elevator up four floors to our Hollywood hotel room. I silently answer my own unintended double entendre, as if the reservations extend to our relationship. *Emotional constipation. Dream throttling. That I'll get too comfortable and everything will come crashing down around us.*

Jamie, fortunately, takes my words at face value. "You'll see. But you're going to want to dress up." He puts an arm out to hold the door while I exit the elevator. He's so considerate. I never consciously noticed what good manners he has, but now that we're boyfriend and girlfriend his latent chivalrous streak has come to the fore. Another thing that's changed between us.

"Then it's someplace fancy," I say, hoping for more clues. Dressed up in L.A. could mean a ball gown or heels and jeans.

"Not exactly. But you can't have too many options in that bag of yours."

"I admit, packing was kind of a nightmare." I like having my entire closet at my disposal, so narrowing down outfits took me most of last night.

"Oh, wow!" I can't help the exclamation as we enter our room and take in the trendily spare furnishings and the heavenly view from the big picture window. The entire city seems laid out at our feet, palm trees and billboards and the sun setting like slowly melting orange sherbet over the Pacific way in the distance.

"You like it?" Jamie asks.

"You're spoiling me." I'm inexplicably nervous. Expensive hotel rooms and taking me out in fancy dress—these are new horizons for our relationship. We used to pay our own way for everything, but now there are gray areas. Neither of us exactly makes bank at our jobs, doing the highly appreciated and fairly compensated work of teaching children (ha), but Jamie owns his home and his family has money, not to mention that he's successfully licensed some of his inventions. The tab for this isn't a big deal to him, in other words. But it is to me, and I hate the power imbalance that implies. He's only two years older than I am, but sometimes I feel like he's a genuine adult, with the bank balance to match, while I'm still one of those stereo-typical millennials who can barely afford both my rent and my health insurance.

"I'm trying to," he says lightly. "You don't make it very easy."

I force my shoulders to relax. "Thanks, it's gorgeous."

"So are you."

I wrinkle my nose. "That was so cheesy."

He laughs. "But not untrue."

"I better change," I say quickly. When he compliments me, all my carefully built emotional armor disassembles itself and I basically want to curl up in his lap and never leave.

"You take the bathroom. I'll change out here," he says. It's nice of him to give me privacy. He knows me so well.

I grab a few items from my suitcase and the shopping bag from the lingerie store and escape to the bathroom. Five minutes later, I've refreshed myself and my makeup, but have run into a minor obstacle.

"Jamie, do you have some scissors?" I yell through the closed bathroom door.

"Yeah, right here," he calls back instantly.

"Really?" I'm surprised.

"No, Ophelia, I did not bring my sewing kit on our weekend trip to Los Angeles," he says dryly.

I giggle despite myself. "Do you have anything sharp? Nail clippers?"

There's a short pause then a knock on the door. I open it a crack and reach out. Jamie presses a pair of small nail clippers into my palm. I'm about to yank my hand back in, when his hand curls over mine.

"Hey, is everything okay? Can I help?"

I glance down at my body and sigh. "I guess so." I open the door wider so he can enter. The look on his face when he sees what I'm wearing is highly gratifying, even if I'm slightly shy about my attire. I've got on a sheer violet lace bra that barely covers my nipples, and a matching pair of violet lace boy shorts. The contrast between the coverage on the bottom and the exposure on the top is pretty fucking sexy, if I do say so myself.

"I got these today while you were in your meeting, and now that they're on, I can't reach the tags. Can you snip them off for me?"

I turn my back and watch him in the mirror over the sink. He's already dressed in dark jeans, his favorite lace-ups, and a hunter green button-down that fits him like a glove. He's taking his time, fumbling a little with the clippers, tracing his fingers over my back. I shiver at the touch. He still hasn't said anything.

"Do you like it?"

"Very much." His voice is low and serious. I shiver again.

He's so much taller than me, so much broader. I feel petite in my bare feet. But not vulnerable. I feel surprisingly strong, even powerful, and very, very sexy. I wait until he manages one snip, then the other, his fingers lingering on lace. The clippers drop to the counter, the tags float away. I lean back, pressing my nearly naked self against his fully clothed front.

I gasp when the unmistakable ridge of his erection presses against my lower back. His hands rise to my shoulders to hold me in place. We stand together, back to front, our reflections in the mirror exposing our desire. Jamie is silent, but I can feel his hunger. Unhurriedly, I grind my ass against him, against his delicious hardness.

"Fuck, O."

Two syllables, uttered like a plea, and I feel myself dampening between my legs. My new panties aren't going to last very long, but I can't bring myself to care. I shift forward and brace myself on the vanity. His hands come down to cup my breasts roughly and now I'm the one moaning.

He flicks the barely-there fabric down so I'm fully exposed, then rubs my nipples ruthlessly with his thumbs. I'm almost embarrassed to be able to see everything he's doing in the too-bright bathroom light, in the too-large bathroom mirror. I can't escape how completely wanton I look, practically naked with my crimson-painted mouth open as I pant with arousal. I have nowhere to hide, no way to avoid seeing how badly I want him, how easily he's able to get me wet and needy.

Jamie watches us, too, his glasses framing eyes that are honed in on my reflection. Every pass of his thumbs over my nipples has me twitching and the ache between my legs is almost painful. I rock back against him, but his hard length is nowhere near where I need it.

"What do you want, Ophelia?"

Not fair. He knows what I want. I let out a whimper.

"What do you want?" he says again, voice like sandpaper. He's going to make me say it.

"You," I cry. "You inside me."

He grasps my breasts one more time, and then his gaze

locks on mine in the mirror and his eyes, dark and unreadable, hold me there while his hands drop away from my body. I hear the zip and the rustle of his jeans and then his cock, lava hot and rock hard, is pressed against the seam of my ass and I'm writhing desperately. It already feels so good.

"Please." I'm not sure what I expect, but it's not for him to simply yank my panties aside and press the blunt head of his cock against my opening.

Even though I'm soaking wet, it still feels incredibly tight as he presses all the way into me. He lets out a ragged cry that tells me he feels it, too. Then I shift and everything slides smoothly again like we're parts of a well-oiled machine made to be connected this way.

I sigh in relief as the need that's been building inside me is partially assuaged by the pulse of Jamie thrusting in and out, but my arousal gains a fresh wave every time I get the courage to watch us in the mirror. Watching him, still mostly clothed, his eyes resolutely open, taking in everything from the bounce of my breasts to the slap of our bodies coming together ratchets up every sensation to eleven.

But my orgasm hovers out of reach. "Jamie. I need—" He's already moving—his fingers rub my clit with the same relentless attention that he paid my nipples. My orgasm rips through me as I let out a cry so loud they must be able to hear it in the lobby.

"Jesus, O." He might be saying more, but I can't take it in, since I'm still coming. My world has shrunk to the fullness inside me, the pressure of Jamie's clever fingers on my clit, and the debauched picture of my barely recognizable self in the mirror.

Finally, Jamie tenses and groans and stutters out my name as he reaches his release.

A long minute passes where I try to catch my breath and it

sinks in that we had dirty, messy, incredible sex in our hotel bathroom.

For some reason I feel shy as Jamie finally meets my gaze in the mirror. His face is so serious. I rearrange my bra so I'm covered up again, as much as I was before. He grabs a washcloth from the vanity and slips out of me, offering me the cloth so I can clean myself up.

My panties are unwearable now, but I don't want to take them off while Jamie's still there putting himself back together. He's strangely silent. Usually I can't get him to shut up after sex about how great and wonderful and amazing it was. I swallow. Did I do something wrong?

"Um, I'll just finish getting dressed," I say hesitantly.

"Sure," he says gruffly. He leaves me alone in the bathroom, the door clicking shut behind him.

I strip out of my ruined underwear and clip the tags off another pair with the clippers, then don a black skirt and blouse combo, throw on some low heels, and fix my somewhat rumpled hair. I look good—dressy, but not too dressy—and my skin has the glow of the recently orgasmed.

But something feels off. Is it because as close as Jamie and I are, and as intimate as what we did is, we haven't been able to let go of a layer of self-preservation? There's something transparent, impenetrable, and ultimately suffocating as plastic wrap around us. Is he keeping me at arm's distance or is it the other way around?

Or am I unsettled because that was the hottest sex I've ever had, and we didn't kiss each other once?

CHAPTER 33

JAMIE

We leave the hotel on foot, heading south on Highland.

"I didn't exactly wear my walking shoes," Ophelia mutters as we dodge a questionable puddle on the sidewalk.

"It's not far." I wrestle a smile onto my face and try to shake the weight off my shoulders.

Here's the thing. Having scorching sex with your super hot girlfriend isn't supposed to make you feel like going a round with a speed bag. But my frustration is the culmination of one thing after another. Ophelia pulls me in close, then pushes me away, and I'm getting a little tired of the routine.

Still, I promised her a fun weekend, and I need to get over myself and deliver.

"I thought we had dinner reservations?" Ophelia's expression is adorably befuddled as we approach Sunset Boulevard and the Arclight Hollywood with its signature silver dome.

"Technically, we do have reservations. Tickets for the eight o'clock show of that indie romance you wanted to see. Dinner's on me—all the popcorn and hot dogs you can eat."

She's been quiet since we left the hotel, but Ophelia perks

up when she realizes I've faked her out regarding our evening's plans. She laughs and throws herself into the game of fancy outing to the movies, and I play along until my smile is no longer forced. We imagine the ticket taker is a snooty maître d' and pore over the snack bar menu as if we're dining at a fancy French restaurant.

"I believe I'll start with the buttered popcorn, and for my entree, a hot dog, with mustard on the side," she says in a faux transatlantic drawl.

"And for the lady's beverage? Root beer or beer beer?"

She pretends to deliberate. They have wine and cocktails, but nothing goes with a hot dog like a cold beer, which is what I know she'll choose.

I order two of everything and a box of Junior Mints for dessert.

We turn our leather recliner seats into a picnic spot. Before the Arclight employee makes her pre-show announcements, I impulsively lean over and kiss Ophelia on the mouth. She tastes salty but smiles into the kiss. I pull away reluctantly. My attention is split between what's on the screen and on the complex, maddening girl sitting next to me. Maybe things aren't as dire as they seem.

My good mood lasts for about thirty minutes into the movie. It's a romantic drama about a woman involved in several ill-fated love affairs. There's a proposal scene, which the woman accepts even though everyone can tell he's a terrible choice for her. I'm fed up with the character's ill-advised decisions. Maybe Ophelia wants to bail on the movie, too. We could go kill time next door at Amoeba Records or head back to the hotel. I can think of a few ways we could spend the rest of the night. Most of them involve O's jaw-dropping choice of undergarments.

But when I glance at her face, she seems into the film, so I resign myself to suffer through the rest. The movie ends with the woman on her own, stronger, but having lost the love of the one guy who was good for her.

"So, what did you think?" Ophelia asks as we wind our way out to the street. Sunset Boulevard is lit up almost as bright as day with all the billboards and car headlights as Friday night cruisers pack the four lanes bumper to bumper. I'm glad we walked.

"It was okay. I didn't really like the ending."

"I knew you wouldn't." There's a smile in her voice.

"What? Why do you say that?"

"You only like when movies have unequivocal happy endings."

"That's not true." At least I don't think it is.

"Oh, please, you're the king of happy endings." She says it like it's a bad thing.

"I appreciate characters who don't make bad decisions and sabotage their own happiness just to serve some dumb writer's plot."

"Sometimes a movie doesn't want to have the same six plot points as every other movie."

"I didn't think the main character was that likable."

"And all female movie characters need to be likable?"

"No. But this one seriously wasn't."

"I enjoyed it. She didn't sacrifice her goals for a relationship. That's why she ends up moving to Paris to run her own art gallery at the end. That *is* a happy ending."

"But she lost her chance to be with that painter, what's-his-name."

"I think it's refreshing to have a female character choose her career over a man."

I know when I've been beaten. "Okay, you win, that is refreshing. Let's talk about something else."

"You want to go to Amoeba?" she asks, giving me an out.

"Definitely."

* * *

"I've shopped more today than I have in the last six months put together," Ophelia says as we wait to check out with our handful of used CDs.

"I've eaten more junk food today than in the last six months put together."

We glance at each other and laugh. Neither of those things is remotely true.

"I'm having fun, Jamie."

"Me too."

Our date is turning out okay after all. It's on the tip of my tongue to say what's been on my mind all night—all week—okay, for what seems like forever, but we get ushered over to a free cashier and the moment passes.

Back on the street I ask Ophelia if she wants to get a nightcap somewhere, but her answering yawn indicates no.

"Sorry, guess I'm tired," she says.

We start up Cahuenga Boulevard. "Not a problem. I can think of some ways we can get more use out of our hotel room."

She grins crookedly at me. "Oh yeah?"

"We got off to a pretty good start earlier, but I'd like to try out the actual bed."

"Right. So...you liked that? Before?" Her unexpectedly hesitant voice makes me stop.

"Of course I did. Didn't you?"

"Yeah."

We walk the rest of the way in silence. I'm reconsidering my approach yet again. When faced with new evidence, adjust your hypothesis. Trying to keep my feelings in check must be backfiring if she couldn't tell that I enjoyed one of the best sexual experiences of my life.

When we get to the hotel room, I ask her to sit on the bed

with me. She kicks off her heels and lets out a little moan of relief.

"Here." I gesture to her feet and she swings them up onto my lap. I start lightly rubbing them, which makes her purr like a cat.

"Thanks."

"Anytime," I say solemnly. "O, I want to tell you something, and I don't want you to freak out." She tenses against me.

"That's not exactly reassuring. Tell me already."

"First, I want you to know that today has been really special to me. Getting to spend so much time with you, being tourists, having fun. It's been really amazing."

"Okay."

"What we did earlier, that was even more amazing. Do you even know how insanely beautiful and sexy you are? The image of you in that outfit, in front of that mirror, with my hands on you." The blood is rushing south as I bring back the erotic picture in my mind's eye. "You felt so good. You made me feel so good. I'll never forget it."

She twists her mouth into a smile. "I'll never forget it either."

"And I think I've made a mistake because I've been holding myself back, for weeks. I think that you don't understand how important you are to me. You're not my friend that I'm working out some sexual tension with. You're not just a woman I'm dating. I don't want to pretend anymore."

"What are you saying?" Ophelia's eyes are wide.

The words I'm about to say are simultaneously the most true and the most terrifying words I will ever utter, but I couldn't hold them back if an earthquake was turning the city into rubble around us.

"I'm saying I love you, Ophelia."

CHAPTER 34

JAMIE

"You love me?"

The relief I feel at having it out there is short-lived. "Of course I do." How is this news to her? Haven't I been showing it every time we kiss, every time we make love?

"I love you, Ophelia. Not like a friend. Not like family. Like a man who loves everything about a woman, who loves having sex with her, who loves making her laugh, who loves buying her pie and popcorn."

She tucks her legs underneath her, breaking our point of contact. "Stop. Please. Stop."

She's crying and it's breaking my heart.

"No, that's the problem. I can't stop. I don't want to. I don't want to ever stop loving you. I don't think I can."

The tears falling down her face are not doing my ego any good.

"But—"

"Why can't you admit that being with me is something you want, too? Why can't you let yourself love me?" My heart must have built-in self-defense mechanisms because I feel anger welling up, directing the hurt outward.

"Because I can't. I didn't want this."

"You didn't want me?"

"I didn't want a relationship. Messiness. I didn't want this to be all or nothing."

"Too bad," I snap. "You knew this would happen the first time you kissed me."

"I know! I thought maybe it would be worth it."

Jesus fuck, is she trying to kill me?

"It *is* worth it. Because you're hurting me right now, Ophelia, but it's worth it because I know how extraordinary you are, how good we are together. I want to be there for you and I want you to be there for me."

"We are there for each other. We're friends—"

"Bullshit. We are not friends. We're lovers. We could be so much more than that."

"So what—if I don't tell you I love you back, we're finished?"

"Of course not." At least, I don't think so. "I—I feel like I've been lying to you, and to myself. I care about you more than anyone else on this planet. And if you don't think that you could ever feel the same way about me, then maybe we do have a problem."

She's still crying, and I want nothing more than to pull her into my arms and comfort her and tell her that everything is going to be okay, but I can't. I don't know if it will be.

"Of course you mean something to me, Jamie. You're wonderful, sexy, considerate. Anybody would love to be with you."

"We're talking about *you* right now, Ophelia, not some hypothetical person. Tell me you'll try, that you won't shove me away when I tell you the truth about how I feel."

She opens and closes her mouth as if she wants to speak but can't.

"I swear I'm not going to propose or demand you be the

mother of my children. The future doesn't have to go any particular way."

"Then why can't we go on as we have been?"

"Because I need to be able to say I love you without you making me feel like I'm telling you I have a communicable disease. You're strong enough to hear that I love you. You're strong enough to be loved. You may not think so, but you are."

She frowns, eyes flashing. "What's that supposed to mean?"

"I know your parents did a number on you, but we're not them."

"Don't blame the poor little divorced girl. My parents made their own choices. I'm trying not to follow in their footsteps."

"And you aren't. But at least they could admit they had feelings for each other."

"What do you know about it? Oh, I forgot, you're like the son my dad never had." Her sarcasm cuts through her tears.

My voice gentles. "And you're like the daughter my parents never had. Everyone in Santa Barbara can see how right we are for each other. Why can't you?"

"Yeah, we're stellar together. A match made in heaven." Her snarky tone is a knife sliding right through my rib cage and into my heart. Just like that, my anger flares up again.

"Jesus, Ophelia. Open your eyes. Grow up. We're in a relationship. It's a good one. And if you can't see that, then you're throwing away the best thing that could happen to you."

As it comes out I know it's too far, and not even really what I meant.

"Thank you for explaining my life to me and for knowing what's best, Mr. Kendell. I guess the fact that I have a career and a life of my own counts for nothing. I guess it's good that I didn't get the fellowship so I can stay right where I belong, by my boyfriend's side." She wipes her eyes with the back of her hand and somehow makes the motion mocking.

"You didn't get the fellowship? Why didn't you tell me?"

"I found out while you were at your meeting today."

"I'm sorry."

"Yeah, well, I can always apply next year."

I'm quiet at that. Next year. Another opportunity for her to leave. Maybe she's right. Maybe we don't belong together if I'm going to ask her to give up her dreams so we can stay that way.

The thing is, I'd wait forever if she told me she wanted me to.

My shoulders slump. The fight's gone out of me. "I'm sorry," I say. "I've clearly made a mess of this. But I wanted to tell you that I love you and I did. I love you." I may be furious with her, but what I feel for her is not contingent on her being all sweetness and light.

"Stop saying that." She's staunched her tears and now she just sounds annoyed.

"What do you want me to say? Forget it? That's not how it works, O."

"I don't know."

The hotel room that had previously seemed so sleek and romantic now seems empty and sad.

"Let's go to bed. We can talk more in the morning." It's lame, but I don't know what else to say.

"I want to go home." Her voice is so faint I barely hear her.

"Oh." Of course. She doesn't love me. Why would she want to spend one more night with me?

"I'll pack up, then."

"No, don't bother. I'll order a car. I'm sure there's someone willing to drive up to Santa Barbara right now."

"I'm not letting you take a fucking car service home in the middle of the night." I stand up and start throwing things into my duffle as if each article of clothing has personally offended me. "I will drive you home. You can sleep on the way if you want."

"What about your meeting tomorrow?"

"I'll cancel it. Or drive back. Whatever." My stuff is all packed. It's only her frilly girly things lying around now. How did this night go so spectacularly wrong?

She hasn't moved and I turn to her with exasperation. "Come on."

"Fine." She packs silently and puts her sneakers on in place of heels.

We don't talk on the way home. There's no traffic and the GTI flies along. Less than two hours pass before I pull up outside her place. There's nowhere to park, so I idle in the street and pop the trunk. I unload her bags of books to the sidewalk in front of her house. The trip to the bookstore seems like a lifetime ago.

"You need help getting these inside?" I ask stiffly.

"I'm sorry." Her voice is small.

"Okay." I'm not ready to say more than that. Maybe she's trying to bridge the gap between us but I'm too tired to take the offering. She's going to have to do better than that.

Before she can say anything else, I retreat to my side of the car. "Bye." My emotions are swirling, and maybe I'm hurting her by the way she gets a kind of stricken look on her face. Yeah. I'm a complete shit. But I can't make myself lie to see her smile again. I get in my car and drive away.

CHAPTER 35
OPHELIA

The first thing I do when I get up on Saturday is trip over one of the bags of books from The Last Bookstore that I had left outside my bedroom door.

I hit my bad toe, long since healed but still tender from time to time, lurch over the pile of books, and break my fall with my hands, but not before banging one of my knees on the hardwood floor.

Cursing, I roll into a sitting position and cradle my foot. Tears spring to my eyes, but my face is already so puffy from last night's crying jag I hold them back.

I'm a mess.

It took me ages to fall asleep and now I'm emotionally hung over. The only good news is that because I was supposed to be in Los Angeles all weekend, I have absolutely zero plans today and no one knows I'm in town. I can wallow in my misery all by myself and no one has to know that I've destroyed my relationship with my best friend.

We didn't exactly, explicitly, break up. But the implication is there. Jamie's in love with me. He wants me to reciprocate. I'm apparently too emotionally stunted to do that and he deserves better. Everyone—his parents, my dad—was right all along. I'm damaged, and I've broken both our hearts by starting down a path I knew I had no right to be on.

All I've done is tease Jamie and myself with the idea of what it might be like if we were totally committed to each other. I should have known better—I *did* know better. I knew this was going to happen.

Fuck, I hate being right all the time.

I shrink in on myself, hoping to shrink my pain as well. My throbbing toe doesn't hurt a fraction as much as my heart right now.

From somewhere far away, I hear a vibration. My phone, tempting me with information from the outside world. I leave my ball of anguish long enough to locate my phone. There's a text from Nicole, a cheerful *Hope your weekend is going super! ;)* I respond with an enigmatic emoji, not wanting to ruin her weekend.

There's also an email from Mom confirming her attendance at the mother-daughter portion of the bachelorette one week from today. I can't even think about that potential horror show right now. Finally, there's an email from Mihret at the museum. I click on it, then wish I hadn't.

We got the funding for the maker lab program. All of it. Enough to install labs at every single elementary school in Santa Barbara. Enough for equipment and supplies for two years. Enough to train librarians and teachers to use and maintain the equipment. A stipend for me to oversee everything for a year, which would double my take-home pay. And a stipend for Jamie, too, to advise on the project and do the hardware installation.

We rocked the proposal. We made a plan, a good one, that will bring innovative and exciting technology to thousands of kids. Jamie and I work seamlessly together, between his vision and technical expertise, and my experience with both making things happen in a public elementary school and how the kids and teachers have been using the lab. We know our stuff.

Since I didn't get the fellowship, there's no reason not to take this program and run with it. It would be great for the kids, great for my career as an educator, even great for next year's fellowship application. The only reason not to jump for joy is that I'd have to work with the one person who claims to love me but who more likely hates my guts right now.

Nicole is going to be so pissed at me for throwing this wrench into her wedding plans. Dealing with uncomfortable exes who happen to be the maid of honor and the best man is not going to fit her theme of "elegant whimsy" or whatever crap she finally decided on.

Next weekend is the bachelorette, then the end of school, and of course, Nic's wedding. But the rest of the summer is completely unplanned. Maybe I should stop dreaming about traveling and go do it. I've never been anywhere, so it doesn't matter where I end up, as long as I can be alone.

My life in Santa Barbara suddenly has a giant Jamie-shaped hole. Everywhere I look, I'll be remembering. The movie theater. The park where we eat our lunch. The museum. The beach. Our lives fit together so well here. If we're avoiding each other the city is going to feel very small.

I open a travel booking app on my phone and start scrolling for deals. *Very mature, running away.* I'm not running away, I argue with the voice in my head, I'm taking a vacation. I'll be home for the start of school, in time to implement the maker lab program. Two months apart might be what Jamie and I need to return to merely a working relationship.

My phone screen lights up with an incoming call. Nicole. If I don't answer she'll keep trying until she reaches me.

"Hey," I answer tiredly.

"Honey, is something wrong?" Her voice sends me over the

edge and I start crying. I try to give her a coherent answer, but I feel like I've let her down and cry harder.

"Where are you?" she asks after listening to me blubber for a minute.

I make a sound approaching "home" through my tears.

"I'll be right there."

* * *

"It's not your fault," she says for the third time. We're curled up on the couch. Nicole has thrown a blanket over me and pets my hair softly. She's so calm, it's kind of scary. I feel like she's comforting me on the outside while her mind is somewhere far away.

"It sort of is. I shouldn't have gotten involved with him if I couldn't see it through." If I pile enough shit on myself, maybe I can stay buried under it and not have to deal with the world outside my own misery.

"You guys have only been together for a month. In the normal scheme of things, that's nothing. It's too soon for declarations of love. It took Ricky ages to tell me he loved me."

"Yeah, but were you guys best friends for two years before you started dating?"

"No, but there's a rhythm to these things. Jamie's rushing you and he knows it."

"But don't you think it's better for him to know now that I'm never going to be able to return his feelings?" My stomach lurches. I suppose I should eat something. I haven't had anything since popcorn and beer last night at the movies and my body would probably appreciate a vegetable or two.

"O, can I tell you something?" Nicole stops stroking my hair and I sit up and look at her.

"You're not pregnant, are you?"

She lets out a surprised laugh. "Ha. No. I hope not."

"Okay, good."

"No, it's not about me. We're still on you. Don't try to change the subject."

"Fine." I flop back and return her hand to my head, indicating she should keep at it.

She smiles and starts up again. "I have to tell you something and you probably aren't going to like it."

That sounds eerily like what Jamie said to me last night. Does everyone think I'm emotionally incompetent? I wait for her to break it to me, whatever it is.

"Regardless of his jumping the gun on the telling you he loves you thing, you are crazy if you think you could never love him back. Because I can tell you without a shadow of a doubt that you could. You *do*. You're not giving yourself enough credit. Not only do you love him, but you love him, like, a lot."

"I do?" I whisper. She's talking to me as if I'm a small child, but I guess part of me deserves it. Not to mention she's always been the big sister in this relationship.

"I know you think you've always been just good friends, even extended family. And that's true. But haven't you two always been a little bit more? Haven't you always had a shelf in your mind set aside for Jamie? Hasn't that giant nerd managed to carve out his own particular place in your heart? Doesn't he always make you feel special? That's love, honey."

"But I didn't want this. I wanted to be free. I wanted to be Miss Rumphius for the digital age. I wanted to read books and travel and make the world more beautiful somehow. I didn't want to fall in love and find my horizons shrunk down to the size of my hometown." I had no clue all of this was inside me, but I can't stop it from pouring out. "I didn't want to be married to someone who could decide one day he didn't want to be married to me anymore. I didn't want to have a child and have to tell her that her dad doesn't want to be with me anymore. I didn't want—" and I'm crying again. Nicole holds me until the tears peter out.

"I know, honey. I know." She might be crying a little, too. "But pretend you aren't you for thirty seconds. Think about Jamie and the way he looks at you and the way he treats you. Do those seem like the actions of a person who's going to wake up one day and say, 'Nah, I'm good. I've had enough of Ophelia in my life. I'm out'? Doesn't he seem like the kind of guy who would follow you to the fucking ends of the earth, or wait patiently for you to come back from wherever you need to go? Love doesn't have to shrink your world."

"But my mom married my dad and she had all her options taken away from her. It was only after they got divorced and I went to college that she got back to where she wanted to be."

"Aunt Helen made her own choices, O. It was a different time. And you aren't your mom."

"So why does this feel so scary? If he's really serious about me and we're as good together as he thinks, why can't I just go with it?"

"Love is still scary. I was scared to commit to Ricky. Why do you think it took us so long to get engaged? We saw friends of ours get married too soon, now they're barely thirty and divorced already. We wanted to be sure. Maybe you don't always need eight years to know if you've made the right choice. Maybe Jamie knew after two months. Or two years. Or maybe he knew the first day he met you, on some level." Nicole's words take me back to that Thanksgiving, to turkey and pie and meeting someone who made me laugh, who made me feel like I could be myself.

They—these godforsaken *emotions*—have always been there, between us, not only on Jamie's side.

"You need to stop being afraid and actually own your feelings. It's not always easy to love a Kendell man. They're workaholics and love their mothers a hair too much. Sometimes they have to be reminded about birthdays and anniversaries. But they're worth it. They're smart and sensitive and good in bed. They don't let anything stop them when it comes to the women they love. They'll do anything for us. And that's a pretty nice feature."

Nicole falls quiet and lets me process. After a while she rises off the couch. "I'll make us a cup of tea." She rustles around in my kitchen as I clutch the blanket like a life raft.

She's not wrong. Jamie probably wouldn't do any of the things I'm afraid he'll do. But it's not as simple as my telling him, "I love you, too." That's not what this is about. This is about me letting go of ten years of insecurity and reaching out toward my future with some semblance of confidence. I don't know if I'm entirely ready. But I do know I'm not ready for our time together to be over, and since we aren't technically broken up...

"Maybe I should go talk to him?" I suggest tentatively when she sets down a steaming mug of green tea alongside a piece of toast slathered with avocado.

I'm certain she's holding herself back from smacking me on the head and saying, "You think?" but she only nods and smiles.

"Okay. I can do that." I take a bite of toast and sigh. "This is good. Thank you."

"Anytime, honey."

"So, are you excited for your bachelorette weekend?"

"Oh my gosh, so excited! I have my schedule completely clear from midnight Thursday on. We are going to have so much fun."

"We are." I smile, trying to be the exuberant maid of honor she deserves. Then my smile breaks. "I don't want to lose him, Nic."

She grips my knee reassuringly. "You won't."

I only wish I was so sure.

CHAPTER 36

OPHELIA

After Nicole leaves, I open my phone again and take a long look at the travel app. Then I close it. It's too soon to run. But I leave the app on my phone. Something in me quiets knowing that it's an option.

I take a shower, aware I'm washing away the last traces of Jamie's touch. The memories of our encounter in the hotel bathroom come back as I look at myself in my tiny over-the-sink mirror.

It's been twelve hours since he dropped me off and I miss him like it's been twelve days. When did I start needing him so much? I have a feeling it started a long time before we acknowledged the attraction between us. He's been more than a friend to me for a long time. But I'm not quite ready to name what he's become. It's too big, too terrifying.

I drive over to his place with trepidation, having no idea what I'm going to say when I see him. He's not there. His GTI is nowhere to be seen—he must have gone back to L.A. for his meeting after all.

The doubts creep in immediately. It stings that he can carry on with business as usual while I've been wrung out like a tear-soaked sponge. Maybe he's not as affected by this as I am.

Maybe he was lying when he said he couldn't stop his feelings for me. Maybe I'm suffering all alone.

He's probably in our hotel room right now, relieved he doesn't have to share the space with a difficult, fickle girl who's proven to be much more trouble than she's worth.

I can't cry anymore, so instead I retreat to something that always makes me feel better, no matter how low I get. I head to the beach.

It's a glorious spring day, and I have a big floppy hat in my trunk, so I drop it on my head and plop myself down on a bench overlooking the sand and the water. Saturday surfers, beach runners, kite flyers, about a million dogs, and people of all ages are out enjoying the sun. The Pacific is always cold, but it doesn't stop kids from splashing into the surf and shrieking when the chilly water surges above their ankles.

I'm lost in the pages of my book, a young adult novel I'm thinking of ordering for my library, when one of the many passersby pauses in front of me, casting a shadow onto the pages of my book.

"Ophelia."

"Dad!" My father has his sketchbook in his hand and a paint-splattered fisherman's cap on his head. "Oh, and Dakota. Hi." The silvery blonde at his side smiles warmly at me and I try to muster up the same enthusiasm for her. We've met once before, a dinner that Jamie bravely escorted me to. It wasn't that bad, actually, with Jamie there to smooth the way. He kept the conversation going and we covered all manner of topics from art and design to everyone's opinion of the new doughnut shop on Figueroa. Dakota is nice, and clearly good for my dad, who seemed relaxed in a way I'd never seen him before. But I don't think I'll ever be BFFs with her the way I'm close with Jamie's mom. Oh shit, if Jamie and I don't make it, does that mean I'm going to lose Laura and Rory, too?

I'm thankful my hat and sunglasses hide my cried-out eyes.

"What are you doing here? I thought you and Jamie were out of town this weekend."

Why does everyone have to know every move we make? I guess it makes sense, since Jamie usually spends Saturday mornings eating dry pancakes and drinking bad coffee with their so-called breakfast club. But still, a little privacy would be nice.

"Yeah, we were. Um, I came back early." God, I wish I were a better liar.

My dad's forehead crinkles. "Everything okay?"

"Yeah!" I fake a normal tone. "Everything's fine. Jamie had to stay and work."

Dad and Dakota exchange a look. Dakota says, "I've got to return a phone call. I'll meet you at the car, Andy. Nice to see you, Ophelia."

"You too." I wave, feeling a bit stupid.

Dad sits down on the bench and my shoulders hunch. I can't escape. A year ago he might have pretended not to notice something was up, but now he says, "What happened?"

I don't want him to be disappointed in me, but I have to tell him. "You were right. What you said when we had brunch— Jamie does have deep feelings for me. He told me he loved me last night." That whole episode has taken on a nightmarish quality in my memory. "My reaction was not...ideal."

"I see." Then he's quiet, and I don't know if it's because he doesn't know what to say or if he's waiting for me to elaborate. I guess it doesn't matter. He's trying and that counts.

"I don't understand why everyone could see this but me," I say. "You, Nicole, probably Laura and Rory. You could all see that he was in love with me and that I was going to break his heart. But I feel like mine is the one that's broken. And that's the entire reason I didn't want to get involved in the first place! How could I be so dumb?"

He laughs a little. "You aren't dumb, sweetie. You have to

understand that not every relationship is the same. You've had men, well, boys, fall in love with you before. It's not hard to see why. You're smart, hardworking, beautiful. And you didn't feel the same way about them. It happens. But all it takes is the right person to make falling in love make all the sense in the world." He sighs and sets his sketchbook to the side.

"But it doesn't matter what Nicole or I or anyone says about you and Jamie. All that matters is what you think, what you feel. And if it's not right for you, it's not right. You don't ever have to be with anyone you don't want to be with. And that's okay. We'll all support you. You don't have to do anything you don't want to do. Maybe he's not what you want."

Wow, after Nicole basically telling me what I felt and my own self-castigation, hearing my dad say maybe Jamie's not the one for me after all is like a bucket of ice water thrown in my face.

"Oh my God, Dad. You are a genius."

"Thank you," he says gravely. "Why's that exactly?"

"Knowing I have the option to say 'This is not what I want' has made me completely realize that it *is* what I want. Is that reverse psychology? Because it fucking worked!"

"Wait, what?"

"I'm in love with Jamie and I want to be in his life. And I have no idea what that means, but it's the only thing that feels right."

"And what I said made you come to that conclusion?"

"Absolutely!"

"Huh." He looks pleased, and a bit befuddled. I lean over and kiss him on the cheek, and his smile widens.

"I need to make a plan."

"For what?"

"You'll see. I'm probably going to need your help. Dakota's, too. But right now, I'm going to the library."

CHAPTER 37

Never a Bride(smaids)

OPHELIA

Hey bridesmaids. I have to ask you all a huge favor. I ran it by Nicole and she said it's OK, but this is going to involve all of you.

KATE

What's up? How can we help?

I sort of need to use the bachelorette weekend to stage a surprise grand gesture to show Jamie that I love him & I'm committing to be with him

ROSIE

What! You love him!?!

KATE

Wow, that's huge!

LANI

Another bridesmaid falls

You know at this rate, Nicole's going to get her damn wish to see us all paired off, right?

ROSIE

Yeah, sorry about that again

I know. Sorry

KATE

Don't apologize. The whole point of the Never
a Brides is that we're there for each other—we
don't shame each other for wanting to stay
single, and we're not shaming each other for
falling in love

Right, Lani?

LANI

Yes, fine, you're right

Jamie is a really lucky guy, O

KATE

By the way, I'm in for the whole grand gesture
thing. If Nicole says it's OK, then we can make
this happen

Thanks. I haven't been very honest with myself
about this. It helps that I can be honest with
you girls.

I'm not saying I'm not scared, but when you
know, you know. Except when you're too
much of an idiot to know you know. But now I
know! I have to tell him & it has to be big. I'm
always keeping to the edges & hiding behind
books & keeping my mouth shut when what I
really want to do is tell everyone how freaking
happy I am

LANI

What are you talking about? You never keep
your mouth shut

ROSIE

Lani!

lol OK, that's fair. But I'm saying Jamie deserves to know how much I want to be with him. And I want everyone to be in on it.

KATE

What do you have in mind?

It's going to involve the museum, 3D printers & a lot of texting

* * *

OPHELIA

You up?

JAMIE

Yes

Back from LA?

I got back last night. I should have let you know, but it was late.

It's OK

Did you see Mihret's email about the funding for the program?

Yeah, great news, right?

…

I noticed you didn't respond to it, though. Everything OK?

I think it's going to be. I'll email her tomorrow.

OK

I've been doing a lot of thinking. I need a few days on my own, if that's OK

Of course, if that's what you need

I'm sorry for overreacting the other night

                    Don't be. But can I ask you for a favor?

Of course

                Give me this time. Alone. Things have been
                moving fast

I can do that. It won't be easy.

                      You're strong. You can make it

You're strong, too, you know

                                I know

                          I'll be in touch

When?

Nicole's Bombshell Bachelorette Weekend
Schedule of Events

Friday

3PM Gather at Nicole's

3PM-5PM Cocktails and dress-up

5PM Depart for dinner at Blackbird

6PM Dinner and cocktails

9PM Dancing at State Street clubs

12AM Return home

Beauty sleep

Saturday

11AM Brunch

1PM Spa Day with Moms

Manicures

Pedicures

Facials

*5PM The *other* Kendell-Winesap couple special event*

6PM - 10PM Beach party and Dinner

Sunday

10AM Brunch

12PM Farewells

CHAPTER 38

OPHELIA

The pop of the cork causes the room to erupt into cheers. "Let's get this epic bachelorette weekend started!" Kate shouts as she pours us all too-full glasses of bubbly.

I'm nervous and excited, and the whirl of activity and girl energy makes me giddy. Pop music blares out of Nicole's multi-room sound system. Kate plies us with drinks and snacks, even though we're all going out to dinner in a little while. Rosie looks the opposite of her usual conservative doctor persona in a pretty sundress, her hair blown out into soft waves, though the expression on her face as Lani brushes glitter over her eyelids is fairly Rosie-ish in its skepticism. The dining room table is covered in shimmering bits of paper, sparkly fake jewels, and tons of makeup, as we're all expected to adorn ourselves with bling before going out on the town.

Rosie and Kate, and by that I mean mostly Kate, have planned all this, bless them. All Lani and I had to do was contribute to the pot to cover food and supplies and promise to be halfway enthusiastic about all the goofy stuff they have in store for the weekend. Nicole made them swear to keep it classy, but we could tell she wanted a big blowout, so I'm willing to endure some mortification to fulfill her fantasy bachelorette bingo card.

Since Nicole is the first one in my admittedly small circle to get married, I wasn't sure what to expect, but this is, in a word, fabulous. It's girly and glittery and decadent and silly, and I start to enjoy myself despite my shredded nerves over what's coming tomorrow.

Nicole seems well on her way to becoming trashed, so I hand her a glass of water so she can survive until the clubbing portion of the evening. She plops down on my lap, disrupting my careful application of sticky gems to the back of my hand in an intricate star pattern.

"I love you, Ophelia!"

"You need to hydrate." I shove her off my lap and settle her on a vacant chair next to the temporary tattoo station.

"And you and Jamie are going to make up and get married and have lots of babies."

"Shut up, Nicole," Lani says from across the table. "I thought you wanted them to get back together."

"We aren't technically broken up," I say. "And I have no idea if we're going to get married or have babies. We'll figure it out." I believe that now. But I'm starting to think my grand gesture idea is stupid. Why have I been putting this off when I could have gone to his house and told him how I felt any day this week?

I glance around at these women who have become my friends over the past few months, including Nicole, my best friend and my sister in truth, and suddenly it doesn't seem stupid. I finally understand why Nic is making such a production out of her wedding, when she and Ricky could have had some quiet, tiny ceremony and their lives afterward would be exactly the same. They want to celebrate the fact they found each other and are building a life together. They want to show off a little and make memories that will last forever. They understand, more than most, that love isn't finite—that all the love they have for each other can be shared and multiplied and enhanced by the love they have for their friends.

"You're pretty smart," I say to Nicole, as she attempts to put on a bride-to-be tattoo upside down on her arm. I correct its orientation and press a wet cloth over the paper against her skin.

"Thank you, honey," she says, pressing her hand against mine. "Why's that?"

"I'm happy you're getting married, and I'm seriously happy that you roped all of us into practically getting married with you, because I'm incredibly lucky to have all of you here to support me when I need it."

"Stop, you're going to make me cry!" Nicole dabs at her eyes. "Is this glitter eye shadow waterproof?"

"Don't worry, we can reapply," Kate says. "For the record, I'm happy that we're here to celebrate Nicole, but I'm thrilled we can help you, Ophelia. You and Jamie, it's sort of like a fairytale."

"Really?" I frown and peel the backing of Nicole's tattoo carefully away. "I'm not familiar with the fairytale that features an emotionally constipated children's librarian and an attractively nerdy inventor."

"For Jamie, it's love at first sight. He sees you, he loves you, but he can never have you. You're his cousin's girlfriend's cousin. It's weird. Plus, he's already in a relationship."

I wrinkle my nose at the reminder that Jamie used to belong to someone else. Kate laughs and jumps onto the couch, taking center stage. She goes on, voice getting more dramatic as she reenacts our little love story.

"He becomes your friend, your confidant, yet he never stops loving you. He's willing to be your friend, forever, never asking more in return. Until one day, it turns out the beautiful Ophelia has a secret kinky side and maybe she wants more from her platonic life partner. It's beautiful."

"Yeah, just like Cinderella," Lani says dryly. "Sex toys bring everyone together."

"So what's your favorite vibrator, O?" Rosie asks.

"Rosie, bad girl!" Nicole giggles, then sobers on a dime. "Yeah, seriously, though, any recommendations?"

My face heats up. An hour and two bottles of champagne into this weekend and we're already on vibrator talk. I mentally shrug. I guess that's why we're here.

"It depends on what you're going to use it for..."

* * *

The rest of the night passes in a haze of alcohol, glitter, music, food, dancing, and more glitter. We must make quite the sight, tripping down State Street in our bedazzled finery, hitting up one club after another.

It's nearing midnight, another shot of vodka can't dull the ache of my feet in my too-high heels, and even Nicole is dragging, her Bride-to-Be tiara tilting precariously on the top of her head as she grinds with some random guy. Lani's lost to the music, dancing with no one in particular, while Kate's hot and heavy with a guy who followed us from the last club. I use my girl-to-girl telepathy to ask Kate if she wants us to intervene and tell him to get lost, but she seems to be into him. He's pretty hot, and so far seems respectful and not too drunk, so I let her have her fun.

Rosie is our designated sober person—she's dancing a little but also making sure we chug more water than booze and is now holding down a table laden with our purses and jackets. Nic's college friends met us at the first club, punked out after the second, and told us they'd see us tomorrow, depending on the size of their hangovers.

"Should we wrap this up?" I ask Rosie. She nods wearily, and I corral the others. Lani comes readily enough, but Kate's got her tongue down the hot guy's throat and I'm hesitant to interrupt. Instead, I grab Nicole. "Time to go home, Nic."

I expect her to put up more of a fight, but she must be tired, because she nods and lets me guide her to the table.

"The car will be here in five," Rosie says. "Where's Kate?"

"Uh, she's occupied," I say, nodding my head to where she's still entwined with the, ahem, gentleman on the dance floor.

"Jesus. I'd say so. Should we tell her?"

"You go," I say.

Rosie sighs and makes her way over to Kate. They talk for a minute, and then Rosie returns. "She says she'll make her own way back."

"Is that a good idea?"

Rosie shrugs. "She's not that drunk. I think she'll be okay."

We bundle Nicole into the car and sing "Dancing Queen" at the top of our lungs the entire way home.

CHAPTER 39

JAMIE

"I'm not really in the mood," I say for the fifth time tonight.

"James, it's my bachelor party. Suck it up and help me celebrate." Ricky drains his lowball glass with a happy sound.

"This isn't a bachelor party, it's bachelorette party counter-programming," I grumble.

Nicole and her bridesmaids are off doing God knows what, and Ricky and I are holding down a dark corner booth at the new whiskey bar in the Funk Zone while Gus, Rosie's boyfriend, gets the next round. Ricky could have made a bigger thing out of this—there are three more groomsmen in addition to me—but I'm relieved they aren't here.

"Oh, I'm sorry, would you rather be sulking in your workshop while you fixate on Ophelia out dancing all night?"

I choose to ignore this, since I figure he's being rhetorical.

"When is this wedding again? You guys have been engaged fucking forever." I'm being pissy, but I'm entitled. I haven't seen Ophelia since the night I drove her back to Santa Barbara. We texted once, and I've been copied on professional emails regarding the maker lab program. But that's the extent of our contact and I'm going through serious Ophelia withdrawal.

"Seventy-one days until the wedding. And if you think I know the exact number of days because Nicole's announcing it every morning in her Instagram Stories or something, she's not." Ricky smiles with sickening self-satisfaction. "It's because *I'm* counting down the days until I can call her my wife."

"Dude. You guys are..."

"Disgustingly adorable? Wildly in love? Meant for each other?"

I sigh. "All of the above." I don't usually find happiness so depressing. But Ricky and Nicole's relationship seems to get stronger the longer they're together. It's what I've always wanted for myself.

"Look, I'm not trying to rub it in how happy we are." Ricky shrugs. "Okay, maybe a little. I'm trying to wake you up, cos. You can have this, too."

"We're all having this, brother." Gus places three fresh glasses on our table and slides into the empty spot next to me. "Fourteen-year-old single malt Scotch. Cheers and felicidades!"

"Felicidades," I echo, and we clink glasses. The smoky alcohol tastes smooth and burns a little on the way down. The pain is worth it. This stuff is more than palatable.

"Good pick, Gus," Ricky says, "but I wasn't talking about the whiskey. I was trying to give Jamie some light at the end of the tunnel. Ophelia isn't going to break up with you. Trust me."

"Do you know something I don't? Because last I checked my girlfriend told me she didn't want to see me for a while. Not exactly a promising sign."

Gus grimaces. "I've been there, man. But I'm with Ricky. You guys can work it out. Rosie told me Ophelia hadn't dated in something like three years before you? Maybe she has to get used to being with someone."

He's not telling me something I didn't figure out for myself, about six hours too late. I was sitting in inexplicable four a.m. traffic on the way back to Los Angeles after dropping Ophelia at home. My plan was to get a little sleep and then make my meeting. I didn't want my plans derailed by my imploding social life.

Then I had my pathetic little epiphany. I have goals, dreams, and I didn't want to set them back just because Ophelia didn't feel the same way about me as I feel about her. I could finally see why she wouldn't want our relationship to interfere with her plans and dreams either.

Not to mention we haven't actually been dating that long. Fucking moron. Why did I have to push?

"I'm giving her space. I'm waiting for Ophelia. Again."

"You need to be thinking about phase two." This from Ricky. Smug bastard.

"Phase two?"

"You know, when she comes around and you guys get back together. How are you going to keep her?"

"Hey, we are technically not broken up, so there's no getting back together. We're still together." I sip my whiskey. "Until I'm informed otherwise, that is."

"Relax, Jamie." Gus nudges my shoulder with his. "She's still your girl. When you're around, the only person she sees is you."

"She does?"

"The first time I met you—remember at this dude's engagement party?" Gus glances at Ricky, who salutes with his glass. "Ophelia barely said two words to me that night, but I distinctly remember her laughing at all your lame inventor jokes. I figured you two were already together, until Rosie set me straight on that score."

"He's right, James. Ophelia does always laugh at your jokes. It's a classic tell."

"But—"

"Seriously, everything is going to be okay." He's starting to sound impatient with me, and I feel slightly guilty for pulling down the vibe of his pseudo-bachelor party, but I'm desperate.

"How do you know?"

"I know because in seventy-one days I'm marrying Nicole Winesap. And you are my best man and Ophelia is her maid of honor and there is no way that Nicole Winesap would let someone else's romantic problems ruin her wedding party. Believe me, you and Ophelia will be happy as clams by the twentieth of June, if not before."

Strangely, this cheers me up. He's not wrong. And if I benefit from Nicole's machinations, I won't complain about her micromanaging ever again. If Ricky and Gus are right, then maybe I should be thinking about phase two and how to show my girlfriend that we can be together without having to sacrifice our dreams. I have a small idea of how to do it.

CHAPTER 40

OPHELIA

I wake up with a headache and it takes me a minute to remember why. No matter how much we tried to stay hydrated, we knew we'd be a little worse for wear in the morning, which is why we are having brunch delivered so late that it really qualifies as lunch.

Today is the day. The day I'm going to tell Jamie how I feel. I'm as nervous as if it were my own wedding day.

I glance at my phone and let out a little yelp. The main event isn't for seven hours. Why am I putting myself through this again? Oh right, because I don't want to screw up my second chance. *Stick to the plan, Ophelia.*

I don't have much time to dwell, anyway. We get up in waves —even Kate, who's magically reappeared during the night. By the time I get my turn in the shower there's a film of glitter on the subway tile of Nicole's guest bathroom. The food arrives, and that, along with coffee and a bottle of ibuprofen we pass around, perks everyone up.

We tease Kate about her display on the dance floor, and she seems a little embarrassed but also a little proud about her hookup, though she's tight-lipped about details. I suspect that's because she can't remember many of them. We drink more coffee, and Lani breaks open another bottle of champagne for the adventurous few who want a mimosa.

Then we steel ourselves for the next event.

It seemed like a good idea when Kate floated it a few months ago. Nicole wanted her mom, my aunt Sandy, involved in the weekend so Kate reached out to her. Somehow that snowballed into including *all* the moms of the bridesmaids and having a mother-daughter spa day. I thought my mom would think the idea was dumb, but she readily agreed. She knows how forceful Nicole can be when she wants something.

Shortly after noon our intimate girls weekend is crashed by the arrival of four middle-aged women. Aunt Sandy gets here first, since she lives about five minutes away. She brings a huge bouquet of flowers and a dozen double pains au chocolat from Helena Avenue Bakery, which wins her points from everyone.

Next to arrive is Kate's mom, Judy, who lives in Los Angeles, like her. She has her daughter's pale skin and wide, open smile, though her red hair is less natural and more salon-induced.

Lani's mom is small and friendly, with jet-black hair untouched by gray. Kaia comes to visit a couple of times a year from Hawaii, so she arranged this trip to coincide with the bachelorette party.

"You're a brave woman," I say when I meet her. She smiles and nods toward Nicole.

"Your cousin is a force of nature. Lani's loved working with her. And since Lani's dates never last longer than a weekend, I figured I should come get my bridal fix while I can." I raise my eyebrows at her blunt assessment. I wonder if my mom feels the same way. Are our generation's mothers girl-power feminists on the outside while secretly hoping for their daughters to have frothy, traditional weddings?

Rosie's mom died when she was young, so her boyfriend's mom shows up for her today.

"So nice to meet you, Mrs. Cuevas."

"Sandra, please," she says. "Mrs. Cuevas is my mother-in-law." She's as quick to smile as Gus and has an opinion about everything, from the quality of the pastries to the likelihood of rain later in the day and seems thoroughly delighted to have been invited. Rosie looks rather emotional at having a mom-type to call her own.

We eat pains au chocolat and prepare to shuttle over to the spa for our manicure and pedicure appointments. I text a few people to confirm that everything's ready for what's happening later today. But my mom still hasn't shown up.

OPHELIA

On your way? Leaving for the spa in 10

No answer.

I try not to be annoyed. Just because I've had more honest communication with my dad in the past few weeks than I'd had in the last ten years doesn't mean my perfunctory relationship with my mother has automatically gotten better.

Once I was installed in campus housing at UCSB, Mom didn't waste much time in putting the house on the market and moving to Malibu. She always loved the beach, but Santa Barbara's a little provincial for her. She likes to be surrounded by new and shiny things, whereas I'm attracted to a more vintage aesthetic. In high school she always tried to dress me in Banana Republic and Ann Taylor while I wanted to troll the thrift shops.

We get along well enough. I know my mother loves me, but she has her own life, and I'm more of a bit player than a main character in it.

She rolls up in a silver two-door BMW as we're getting into two of the moms' SUVs to caravan to the spa. She looks fantastic in white jeans, a striped boatneck shirt, and wedge sandals. Her shoulder-length blonde hair is blown out and her makeup expertly applied. She looks as if she's coming from the spa, rather than on her way there. I sense the other moms exchange glances, perhaps feeling a bit drab by comparison in their casual shift dresses and flip-flops. That's what I'm wearing, too. Who wears jeans to get a pedicure?

Before Mom greets me, she gives Nicole a big hug, and then hugs Aunt Sandy. We all spent nearly every holiday together once upon a time. But those days are long past.

Nicole quickly makes introductions, and Mom greets everyone with a bright smile. Her gaze finally falls on me.

"Hi, Ophelia."

"Hi, Mom." I walk over and give her a hug mostly because I think the rest of the party will think it's weird if I don't.

She hugs me back, and I get a whiff of her perfume. She's always worn Chanel, even when she worked at home managing the graphic design business with Dad. I always associate the smell with her—both expensive and out of place. It's not that Santa Barbara doesn't have unbelievable wealth. My dad's family comes from old money, but he never had any of it while my parents were married. I grew up solidly middle class, while Nicole lived in the foothills and went to private school. I went to a school like the one I work in—made up of students with a range of backgrounds, incomes, and cultures. None of the other moms wore Chanel.

"Time to go, first appointments are in a few minutes," Kate calls, and everyone obediently piles into the cars.

"Let's go in mine," Mom says, taking my arm. "We can talk on the way."

"This is a very zippy car, Mom. When did you get it?" I ask as I strap myself in.

"I love it. I got it with my Christmas bonus." There's a trace of pride in her voice. She's very good at her job, and she gets compensated accordingly. She's enjoying what her hard work brings her. It's great to see her so fulfilled, but it makes me sad sometimes that I figure so marginally in the things that make her happy.

She steps on the gas and the car leaps forward, only to slow down once we hit the inevitable downtown Santa Barbara Saturday traffic.

"So, tell me about this boy, and about the crazy scheme you have cooked up for this afternoon."

She doesn't beat around the bush.

"The boy is Jamie Kendell. You've met him a couple of times, remember?"

"The tall skinny kid?"

"He's not skinny." I wish I didn't sound so defensive. Jamie's hot and I don't have to prove anything to my mother. "He's Ricky's cousin, he grew up in Santa Barbara, he's the head of the maker space at The Fox, and he's also an inventor. He's really smart. Brilliant, actually. He's really important to me."

"And what exactly are you trying to accomplish today?"

Jesus. This feels like oral exams. "I need him to know how much I care about him, and I have to do it this way. Jamie knows I hate public spectacles. He thinks they're romantic."

"I'm not sure I like the idea of you doing something you hate because he likes it."

"It's not exactly like that. I want to do something momentous, something memorable."

"So take him skydiving. Whisk him away to Paris. Give him a blow job."

"Mom!"

"Look, I spent fifteen years trying to live my life to make your dad happy, and in the end, neither of us were. I wasted a lot of time over a man. The fact that you never seemed interested in getting into a serious relationship was always such a relief to me. You are so smart, Ophelia. You know that your dreams are more important than anyone else's. Just because you like this boy doesn't mean you should forget that."

This is activating my buttons on so many levels, I don't even know where to start, but I have to say something.

"I know you and Dad weren't a good fit, and you are both much happier now. But what you never seemed to realize is that there was one person in your relationship who was happy." I'm trying not to cry but about to fail spectacularly. "*Me.* I loved our family. I loved family dinners with you guys and how sometimes you would both walk me to school and going to the zoo together on the weekends. You guys gained your freedom when you split up, but I lost my family. And it's taken me a long time to realize that it's okay to try to build a family with someone else."

"You're not pregnant, are you?" Mom sounds horrified.

"Mom, I'm not pregnant. Fuck. That's not what I mean. Are you even listening to me?" I swipe at my eyes furiously. "Jamie and I are different from you and Dad. We have more in common. We support each other. He loves me, and I finally figured out that I love him back. And maybe that means we both have to sacrifice something. Or maybe we won't have to if we work on it, together. I'm willing to try."

She's silent. She may not believe what I'm saying, but I do. I point to a white stucco building on the corner. "There's the spa." She pulls into the adjoining lot and finds a spot. We've beaten the other cars with Mom's horsepower and exuberant driving, so we idle, not saying anything.

I don't need her to understand. I need her to accept that I'm different from her. I'm about to say words to that effect, but she finally responds.

"I never thought about it that way. Our family, I mean. Your father and I loved you so much, and we took so much joy in you, it made it easier to pretend that things were working out between us, even though I knew early on that I'd made a mistake."

She shifts in her white leather seat to face me. For the first time, I notice lines around her eyes and a groove between her eyebrows that artful makeup can't hide. She's always seemed young to me, but my parents are getting older. Which means I'm not a child anymore. I'm the same age Mom was when she had me.

"But *you* were not a mistake. You are the best thing I ever did, and I hope you know that. You're amazing, Ophelia. You didn't deserve a family that fell apart. I'm sorry that we couldn't give you that."

I take a shaky breath through my nose, afraid to open my mouth lest I start bawling.

"The last few years, watching you build your life and your career, find your footing—it's been so wonderful. Selfishly, I was relieved to see you doing it on your own, not getting distracted by a relationship." She gives me a sad, lopsided smile. "But if this boy...if *Jamie* helps you get where you want to go, rather than holds you back, then I'm happy for you. Really."

I smile tentatively and clear my throat, keeping the tears at bay. "Thank you for that."

"I know we don't hang out as much as other moms and daughters, but I never thought that was something you wanted. You always had Nicole and your other friends. I never thought you wanted to hang out with your boring mom."

"Mom, you aren't boring," I say dryly. "And we should hang out more. I'm sorry, too. I haven't made enough of an effort lately."

"Well," she says briskly moving off the tough topics. "I'm here now, and we're going to spend the day together getting dolled up, and later we're going to show your man that he's chosen the best girl in the world to fall in love with. I'll grill him afterward." She grins at me as I roll my eyes. "I'm joking! Sort of."

"You do what you have to do, Mom. Jamie can take it." I'm just relieved she's transitioned from calling him a boy to a man. Because he is a man. He's my man. And I'm determined to keep him.

CHAPTER 41

JAMIE

ALANNA ALVAREZ

Sorry to bother you on your day off, but we have a problem with the MakerBot Replicator and Nina needs it for her workshop tomorrow morning. Can you come reboot it?

JAMIE

Sure, I'll stop by later

There's an event at 6, so it would be awesome if you could come before then

Understood. It's not like I have anything better to do on a Saturday than come into work!

Just kidding

I don't

Haha. It won't take long. And maybe if you taught some of the other techs how to troubleshoot your baby, you wouldn't have to come in on the weekend

Msg received. See you in a few.

The museum has been officially closed for fifteen minutes by the time I roll up, but I can see through the plate glass front doors that there are still quite a few people milling around inside. They must be here for the event Alanna mentioned, though I don't recall any private events on the calendar for tonight.

I honestly don't mind being called in. The Replicator, one of our largest printers, can be finicky and they're going to need it for tomorrow's demos. I'm more annoyed that I wasn't doing anything more important on a Saturday afternoon than tinkering in my workshop and waiting to hear from my still-MIA girlfriend.

I'm about to use my key, but the museum's entrance seems to be unlocked. I walk into the large open foyer. The first person I see is Mihret. She's talking to Ophelia's dad. That's strange. What is Andy doing here after hours on a Saturday? Dakota's at his side. And there's Helen. I've met Ophelia's mom only a handful of times before, but she looks so much like Ophelia. They share the same bone structure and shade of blonde hair, though she keeps hers shorter.

This is weird.

Then there are a bunch of people from the museum, including Alanna, which is less weird, except most of them are not usually scheduled for the weekend. I continue to see people I know, coworkers and friends, even my parents. Ricky's parents are here, too, and Ricky, on the stairs leading up to the mezzanine. Is this some kind of surprise party for me? My birthday isn't for three more months.

"What's going on?" No one answers me, but everyone looks excited and conversation slowly stops. I glance up at the mezzanine. The bridesmaids are all there, Kate and Lani and Rosie, looking sparkly and smiling hard. And there's Nicole, wearing a plastic crown, for some reason. Then I see her.

Ophelia.

She's the only person in the room besides me who's not smiling and she's the most beautiful person I've ever seen. I don't register anything except her presence. I've missed her so much and it's only been a week. I'm still not quite sure what's going on, but part of my soul is soothed by just being in the same space as her.

"Hi." For openers, it's nothing special, but my brain isn't exactly working at top speed. I'm too busy tamping down the hope that's unfurling in my chest. She wouldn't stomp on my heart in front of all these people. Would she?

"Hi."

"What's up?" I really need to come up with something more eloquent.

"The Replicator isn't really broken, you might have guessed." She seems nervous, her voice shaky, but I can hear it clearly.

"So I gathered."

"And I know you think public proposals are romantic, so I thought..."

This sets off a slight rumble through the crowd. Do they know what they're here for? Do I know what they're here for? I can't let myself go there.

"I've been afraid and I don't want to be anymore. I asked everyone to come here because these people know us, have watched us become friends, and are the reason we've become family." She glances around at the gathering. Nicole wraps an arm around Ophelia's shoulders. She's right. We're a family because of all these threads weaving us together, making something resilient.

"They've supported us as we've taken tiny baby steps toward becoming something else. Sometimes it feels like all these people knew all along what I have belatedly realized." She's so brave. I'm in awe of how strong she is.

"I'm in love with you, James Richard Kendell. I have been

for a long time. I think I always will be. And in front of all these people, I want to say this—I'm always asking what would Miss Rumphius do? She'd grab hold of the best things in her life and make the most of them. Jamie, you are the best thing in my life. You make all the other wonderful parts of my life that much sweeter, richer, brighter. And you do that asking nothing in return. But I want to give you something.

"I want to give you my heart. I've kept it to myself for too long. I was afraid to share it. But I trust you. You won't break it. And I promise, in front of everyone we love, not to break yours."

There's a pause while Ophelia comes down the stairs from the mezzanine, the folks lined up there moving over with grins on their faces. She's got something in her hands and holds it out to me once she comes to a stop about a foot away. Still not close enough to suit me.

"What's this?" I ask.

"It's a heart. I made it in my maker lab." She smiles shyly. "It's for you."

I take the piece and examine it. It is indeed an anatomically correct heart rendered in cherry red plastic.

It's perfect.

"You once said you didn't think you could stop loving me." She looks right at me, her eyes wide and lovely and hopeful. "Well?"

"I can't. I won't. I love you, Ophelia." Then I'm kissing her, the heart squashed between us, a clamor of cheers washing over us, dimly heard over the roar of the blood rushing through my head. I taste Ophelia's tears in our kiss. Or are they mine? Our bodies meld and merge for a long moment. I don't care that our parents or my boss are watching. I need to be as close to her as possible. I murmur nonsensical endearments against her lips, and when we finally pull apart her cheeks are scarlet and I know she needs me as badly as I need her.

A wolf whistle pierces the air and Nicole yells, "Drinks on me to celebrate the happy couple!"

I lean in so only Ophelia can hear me. "Drinks? A party? I need to be alone with you."

"I may not have thought this part through," she agrees. "But I thought you'd appreciate the gesture."

"I do, I definitely do," I say. "And now I need to appreciate your body. In private."

"One hour?"

"One drink," I counter.

"Even better. Let's go."

CHAPTER 42

OPHELIA

Okay, so it all went better than I dared hope—mortifying and scary for me, but so incredibly worth it to see Jamie's smile, proud and surprised and, yeah, a little teary. But it's still a relief when we're able to extricate ourselves from the crowd and be alone.

"There are a lot of people invested in our happiness," Jamie says as we walk the half-mile toward my house, holding hands like teenagers. The fancy cocktails at the tiki bar down the block from The Fox are strong, so we decided not to drive home.

"So it seems."

"Are you happy, Ophelia?" Jamie stops and looks at me. His eyes are bright, glowing even, behind his glasses.

"Happier than I've ever been," I whisper.

"I love you," he says. My heart flips, but not in fear. In excitement. In reciprocity.

"I love you, too." It doesn't feel so strange to say it, now that I've confessed it in front of dozens of people.

Slowly, Jamie places his hand along my jaw, tipping my chin up so my lips meet his in an agonizingly slow kiss. He slides his palm around the back of my neck and tangles his fingers in my hair. My mouth burns from the heat coming off our kisses, which deepen frantically until we yank ourselves apart, gasping for air, bodies on fire with need.

"Home. Hurry." We practically run the last few blocks, until we arrive, laughing and breathless, at my bungalow. Once inside, we attack each other again, mouth to mouth, body to body. It's been too long since I touched him like this and I'm starved for the weight of him on top of me. The bed's too far away; I pull him down to the couch, urging the removal of our clothes, or at least the ones in the way of him getting inside me.

We don't need to talk. What we need is—he enters me in one swift stroke—yes, *that*. I groan at the sensation of him filling me up. I surround him with my heat.

"Jamie, you feel so good."

He kisses me, and stays there, our tongues tangling as he drives into me with stroke after stroke. "I'm not going to last," he mutters, and I don't give a flying fuck, which I tell him. This, for some reason, puts him over the edge, and then I go, too.

Minutes later, I come to my senses, half-undressed, in a puddle of afterglow on my couch. Jamie is stretched out on top of me, his curls tickling my cheek.

"That wasn't exactly how I thought that would go," Jamie says. The rumble of his voice fills me with a delicious feminine satisfaction. He's mine, he's in my bed, well, couch, close enough, and we have the rest of our lives to make each other feel incredible.

"You have something more specific in mind?"

"Actually, I was wondering if you could show me—" he stops and nuzzles his face into my neck as if embarrassed.

"What? What is it?"

"I was wondering if you wanted to use your—toys—sometime?"

"My toys—oh! My toys," I say, thinking of the contents of my bedside table drawer. I haven't used them much since Jamie and I started having sex. "Is that something you'd be interested in?"

"Everything about you interests me." My cheeks grow warmer at the compliment. "And I think I'd be interested in doing anything you wanted to try."

"Anything?" My mind flits to a few kinky ideas.

"Anything," he repeats. "Everything." He's serious.

"That's a lot of things," I tease, trying to keep it light.

"So, what do you say?"

"I'd be honored to show you my modest collection of sex toys, Jamie."

"Right now?"

I'm pretty comfortable but moving to the bedroom seems like a decent idea. "Sure."

We untangle ourselves and head for the door. Jamie's wearing boxers and a half-unbuttoned green checked shirt. I've lost my shoes and underwear and my carefully chosen black and pink sundress is disarranged. I take a moment to remove it. Jamie watches me intently as I stand in only my bra—one of the lacy ones from our ill-fated adventure in Los Angeles. I grab some pajama shorts and put them on, but don't bother with a top. Experimenting with sex toys usually leads to fewer clothes rather than more.

I open my little treasure trove and set some of the items out on the bed. I hold up a pink, oblong object in the vague shape of a penis. I'm not into my toys being particularly anatomically correct. "This is a dildo."

"I know that."

I smile at his defensive tone. "Hey, this is the ultimate safe space, okay? It's just us and some bits of plastic."

"Okay."

I put it in his hand so he can feel its weight. I know the scientific part of his brain will be interested in the specs and I wonder how successful it'll be against the lizard part that's going to want to experience the practical side of things.

"It's made of silicone and it can be used for a few different purposes. In my experience, I like to come with a combination of pressure on my clit and something inside me, so I usually use this vaginally." I'm trying to be clinical in my tone, but Jamie's tenting his boxer shorts as he probably visualizes what I'm describing.

I hold a smooth egg-shaped device. "This is a vibrator. I use it for clitoral stimulation. It has a bunch of modes, but usually the slowest one is my favorite. More realistic." I flick it on and off a few times, feeling my own rush of Pavlovian arousal at the little hum it gives off.

"Huh." Jamie swallows.

I smile. "Shall I go on?"

"Please."

"The lube is pretty self-explanatory. It keeps everything nice and wet. Really important."

"Totally." His voice is hoarse.

I point at a small, curved object with a flared end. "This is a butt plug. I've experimented with it a bit, and I find that I like a little extra fullness sometimes. If you want to try one, we'll get you your own."

"Jesus. We've been sleeping together for weeks and we haven't talked about any of this."

"Things have been going pretty well in that department."

"I thought so, but you seem to know what you like and everything we've done is so vanilla." Jamie seems to be at a loss.

"I know what I like when I'm by myself. We have all the time in the world to explore what we like when it's the two of us."

He sighs. "You're right, but I feel like a moron because I never asked you about any of this before. I thought you'd tell me if something wasn't working for you. Right?"

"What we've been doing has definitely been working for me."

"Me too."

I lean over and give him a soft, lingering kiss. "Everything works. Let's tell each other if there's something else we want to try."

"Yeah." Jamie looks slightly bewildered, and I bite back a smile. He's usually the more experienced and more self-assured one. It's nice to have greater expertise in something for once.

I kiss him again, which turns into long minutes of making out slow and deep. I stretch out on the bed beneath him, arousal making me sluggish and greedy at the same time. It feels sinfully good to have the man I love covering me, caressing me, showing me how much he loves me with every kiss.

I stop kissing him to say, "I feel cherished, Jamie."

He drops his forehead to mine, eyes shut tight behind his glasses. "I love you so much."

"I know."

"I love the heart you made," he says, surprising me with the change in subject.

"Oh. I'm glad." I don't tell him about my first three mangled attempts to get the machine to do what I wanted. "A few of the kids at school helped me. Some of them are way more advanced with the equipment than I am."

"That's awesome."

"Yeah." I think back to Jewel and Taryn giggling when I tried to put the red filament in upside down.

"They were sweet. Actually, they made me realize something. I've been looking for opportunities to leave Santa Barbara, thinking I had to go somewhere new to make the world more beautiful. But to these kids, I've already done that. I've tried to make my library a place where every child who walks in feels safe to investigate and create, not only consume."

I'm half-naked and maybe there's a better time for this conversation, but that's the beauty of being with Jamie—he gets me even when I don't make sense.

"I think this program we're doing is really important. I don't actually have to go somewhere else to make the world a more beautiful place."

"You've certainly made the world more beautiful to me," Jamie says, stroking a hand through my long since tumbled-down hair. "But you can still explore faraway places. I was actually going to ask if you'd mind me tagging along on a trip with you. I could take some time off from the museum this summer —maybe after the wedding? We could pick a spot on the map and go."

His idea echoes my own thoughts. If he comes with me, I'll be able to travel without leaving my heart behind. "I like that idea. How do you feel about North Africa?"

"That would be cool. Or Greece?"

"Ooh, yes. Or—"

"Bali!" we shout in unison. We're on the same page at long last, and I know this time we'll be able to stay there.

EPILOGUE
OPHELIA

"I thought the zoo would be busier on Memorial Day," I say as we traverse the first hill on our way to the big lawns with views of the ocean. We have the entire day to see the animals, and I'm already starving for the picnic lunch we brought.

Luckily, Nicole is in charge of the food, so I know there's more than enough for our small group. Ricky's got the cooler on a wagon and is manfully trudging up the hill towing it behind him. "Wait until later," he says. "The families with the little kids will be out in force."

When we get to the top Nicole says, "Can you get the blanket out, Dakota?"

Dad's girlfriend unrolls the picnic blanket with a flourish. He moves to take out his sketchbook, but Dakota elbows him. "After lunch, Andy."

He acquiesces and helps Ricky pass around bottles of iced tea and lemonade.

"Make me an Arnold Palmer, won't you, dear?" Jamie's mom asks his dad.

"Coming right up," Rory says. "This spread is fantastic."

"Since we finally decided on a caterer, I've been able to cook more," Ricky says.

"But don't let that scare you," Jamie says, the last to arrive on the top of the hill, carrying the most important item of all: dessert.

The ocean sends a pleasant breeze over our party as we sit and eat and talk.

"A little over a month until the big day," Laura says between mouthfuls of pasta salad. "You two ready?"

I know she's talking to Nicole and Ricky, but I glance at Jamie and can't help but think about cementing our relationship with a marriage ceremony someday. The idea isn't entirely abhorrent. But I know we don't have to get married to be in this for the long haul.

"So ready," Ricky says. "I can't wait to have this circus over with so we can get down to the important stuff."

Nicole kisses him on the cheek. "That's sweet. But never call our wedding a circus again, please."

"All I'm saying is we're going to have earned that honeymoon."

"Where are you guys headed?" Dakota asks.

"Paris, of course," Nicole says, beaming.

"Ah, the City of Light," Dad says grandly. "Maybe we should take a trip there, love."

I have to look away from the gooey eyes my dad is making at his girlfriend. I'm happy for them, but a daughter has her limits.

"Rory and I went to Tijuana on our honeymoon," Laura recalls. "We were so broke, but we had fun anyway."

"Except for the part where I haven't been able to drink tequila for the last thirty-five years," Rory adds, to much laughter.

"Are you guys excited about your trip?" Dakota asks, this time to Jamie and me. "I've never been to Bali."

"It's going to be an adventure," Jamie says.

"My passport arrived yesterday," I say proudly.

"Good for you," Dad says, giving me a pat on the shoulder.

My smile feels like it's taking up half my face, but I can't help it. It turns out that once you start acknowledging your emotions, it gets harder to tamp them down where no one can see them. And that's not such a bad thing. In fact, it feels pretty good.

"Where's that dessert, son?" Laura asks.

"The bar is open," Jamie quips, opening the box he'd brought to reveal dozens of different dessert bars, from brownies to salted caramel to lemon. "There's a pecan pie bar with your name on it, sweetheart," he says to me. Then he winks. I swear my heart stops beating for a second. How lucky am I to have a gorgeous, brilliant man offer me my favorite thing besides books and orgasms?

Maybe it's not luck. Maybe it's what I deserve. I thought cutting myself off from sex and love meant protecting myself from getting hurt. Turns out I was deluding myself. Sex isn't the issue. There are things that are more important than sex. Like building a life with the people I love in it. I was really cutting myself off from the fear of losing a family again. What I realize now is that I didn't lose my family. My family changed. It got bigger. It got better.

When the remains of lunch are cleaned up, the dessert decimated, the cooler stashed behind a palm tree for later retrieval, Jamie turns to me. "So, Ophelia, what should we see first?"

I grin and put my hand in his. "Let's go find the unicorns."

* * *

* * *

Thank you for reading!
Scan the code to download a free bonus chapter showing
Ophelia and Jamie's first meeting and read it now!

xoxo,

Libby

ACKNOWLEDGMENTS

With this book I hope to honor children's librarians and those who choose to work with kids. As the mother of two small children, I'm in awe of those who teach them. Ophelia and Jamie take on this task with grace; I could not.

While this book takes place in the real city of Santa Barbara, California, the geography of the city is fictionalized, as are its landmarks and other locations.

Thank you as always to my family, and to all of my writer friends, who seem to have "cheerleader" in the fine print of their job description.

Huge thank you to the expertise of my editing and design team: Sue Khodarahmi, Brian Calvert of Calvert Illustrations, and Dylan Osborn. Each book in this series has been a joy to see come to life.

One of my favorite books, children's or otherwise, is *Miss Rumphius* by Barbara Cooney. It inspired me as much as it inspires Ophelia, and I encourage you to seek it out and give it a read. Have you found something you can do to make the world a more beautiful place?

ABOUT THE AUTHOR

Libby Waterford is the author of the Sawyer's Cove: The Reboot and the Never a Bride series. She's obsessed with her pollinator garden, DIY fermentation, and writing swoony first kisses and hopeful happily ever afters. Her steamy contemporary romances mix witty banter and all the feels with a solid dollop of good old-fashioned sexual tension. Libby wrangles her two ever-growing sons and a husband in Fairfield County, Connecticut.

Get a free story at libbywaterford.com and email her at libby@libbywaterford.com.

facebook.com/LibbyWaterford

instagram.com/libbywritesromance

bookbub.com/authors/libby-waterford

goodreads.com/libbywaterford

amazon.com/author/libbywaterford

tiktok.com/@libbywaterfordauthor